OUTNUMBERED

The moon was up and the small clearing was bathed in light. From down the canyon there was a click of a hoof on stone, a stir of movement, and Russell and his men came forward riding in a tight bunch. There were nine or ten of them. Too many.

Sean's position was excellent. He had fairly good cover, and his body merged with the trees and rocks behind him.

They came on, walking their horses. The shadows from the moon, the trees and weird rock formations made a mystery of the darkness.

"I can smell smoke," Russell said.

"There's a fire," someone else said. "It is almost out."

"You are near enough," Sean spoke in a conversational tone. "Just stand where you are."

Bantam Books by Louis L'Amour
Ask your bookseller for the books you have missed

NOVELS

BENDIGO SHAFTER
BORDEN CHANTRY
BRIONNE
THE BROKEN GUN
THE BURNING HILLS
THE CALIFORNIOS
CALLAGHEN
CATLOW
CHANCY
THE CHEROKEE TRAIL
COMSTOCK LODE
CONAGHER
CROSSFIRE TRAIL
DARK CANYON
DOWN THE LONG HILLS
THE EMPTY LAND
FAIR BLOWS THE WIND
FALLON
THE FERGUSON RIFLE
THE FIRST FAST DRAW
FLINT
GUNS OF THE TIMBERLANDS
HANGING WOMAN CREEK
THE HAUNTED MESA
HELLER WITH A GUN
THE HIGH GRADERS
HIGH LONESOME
HONDO
HOW THE WEST WAS WON
THE IRON MARSHAL
THE KEY-LOCK MAN
KID RODELO
KILKENNY
KILLOE
KILRONE
KIOWA TRAIL
LAST OF THE BREED
LAST STAND AT PAPAGO
  WELLS
THE LONESOME GODS

THE MAN CALLED NOON
THE MAN FROM SKIBBEREEN
THE MAN FROM THE
  BROKEN HILLS
MATAGORDA
MILO TALON
THE MOUNTAIN VALLEY WAR
NORTH TO THE RAILS
OVER ON THE DRY SIDE
PASSIN' THROUGH
THE PROVING TRAIL
THE QUICK AND THE DEAD
RADIGAN
REILLY'S LUCK
THE RIDER OF LOST CREEK
RIVERS WEST
THE SHADOW RIDERS
SHALAKO
SHOWDOWN AT YELLOW
  BUTTE
SILVER CANYON
SITKA
SON OF A WANTED MAN
TAGGART
THE TALL STRANGER
TO TAME A LAND
TUCKER
UNDER THE SWEETWATER
  RIM
UTAH BLAINE
THE WALKING DRUM
WESTWARD THE TIDE
WHERE THE LONG GRASS
  BLOWS

SHORT STORY COLLECTIONS

BOWDRIE
BOWDRIE'S LAW
BUCKSKIN RUN
DUTCHMAN'S FLAT
THE HILLS OF HOMICIDE
LAW OF THE DESERT BORN
LONG RIDE HOME
LONIGAN

NIGHT OVER THE
  SOLOMONS
THE OUTLAWS OF MESQUITE
THE RIDER OF THE RUBY
  HILLS
RIDING FOR THE BRAND
THE STRONG SHALL LIVE
THE TRAIL TO CRAZY MAN
WAR PARTY
WEST FROM SINGAPORE
YONDERING

SACKETT TITLES

SACKETT'S LAND
TO THE FAR BLUE
  MOUNTAINS
THE WARRIOR'S PATH
JUBAL SACKETT
RIDE THE RIVER
THE DAYBREAKERS
SACKETT
LANDO
MOJAVE CROSSING
MUSTANG MAN
THE LONELY MEN
GALLOWAY
TREASURE MOUNTAIN
LONELY ON THE MOUNTAIN
RIDE THE DARK TRAIL
THE SACKETT BRAND
THE SKY-LINERS

NONFICTION

EDUCATION OF A
  WANDERING MAN
FRONTIER
THE SACKETT COMPANION:
  A Personal Guide to the
  Sackett Novels
A TRAIL OF MEMORIES:
  The Quotations of Louis
  L'Amour, compiled by
  Angelique L'Amour

LOUIS L'AMOUR
THE CALIFORNIOS

BANTAM BOOKS
NEW YORK • TORONTO • LONDON • SYDNEY • AUCKLAND

THE CALIFORNIOS
A Bantam Book

PRINTING HISTORY
Saturday Review Press edition published April 1974
Bantam edition / October 1974
23 printings through April 1988

Photograph of Louis L'Amour by John Hamilton—
Globe Photos, Inc.

ISBN 0-553-25322-0

Published simultaneously in the United States and Canada

Bantam Books are published by Bantam Books, a division of
Bantam Doubleday Dell Publishing Group, Inc. Its trademark,
consisting of the words "Bantam Books" and the portrayal of
a rooster, is Registered in U.S. Patent and Trademark Office
and in other countries. Marca Registrada. Bantam Books,
666 Fifth Avenue, New York, New York 10103.

PRINTED IN THE UNITED STATES OF AMERICA

KR   32 31 30 29

To my very good friend,
Mauri Grashin

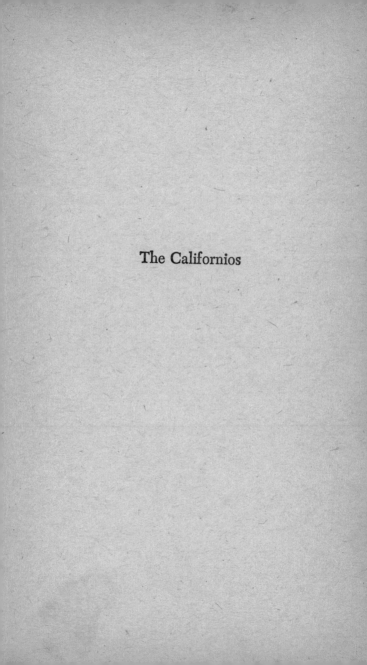

The Californios

Chapter 1

The ranch house on Malibu was a low-roofed adobe with a porch across the front from corner to corner. A door and two windows opened on the porch, both windows showing evidence of being enlarged at some time in the past.

The two large *ollas* that hung from the porch beams contained water kept cool by wind and shade. A gourd dipper was next to them.

To the left of the house, about a hundred and fifty feet away, was a pole corral. Near the corral there was a long watering trough made of rough planks and a lean-to stable.

Shading part of the dooryard was a valley sycamore, a huge old tree with mottled bark, and nearby stood several cottonwoods and another sycamore. Behind the house were several pin oaks. Cottonwoods grew near the door.

The hills around were brush-covered and scattered with huge boulders or sandstone outcroppings. From the porch there was a good view down the winding trail and a glimpse of the blue sea beyond.

Eileen Mulkerin came to the door. The mother of two grown sons, she looked young enough to be their sister, a strikingly beautiful woman, as Irish as her name. "Are they coming, Michael?"

"Not yet."

"They'll not be long, you can be sure of that. It's the day Zeke Wooston has been waiting for ever since your father gave him that whipping for beating his horse."

"He's shrewd . . . and dangerous."

"He is that. It was the Valdez note that surprised me. When he bought it I knew we were in trouble," she said.

"You must not blame Valdez. He did not know Wooston as we know him, and times are hard. He needed the money."

"I do not blame him. He is a good man who thinks ill of no one. He is too sure of the goodness of the world."

They stood together in the late morning sun, looking down the trail. Eileen Mulkerin and her son in his brown monk's robe.

"I wish Sean was here," she said.

"Me, too."

"He is much like his father," she said, "and so are you. But there are things he can do that would not be fitting for a man of the church."

He shook his head. "Now, Señora. You are not thinking of violence? It would do no good, and besides, there is the law."

"Sean would think of something."

"What is there to think? Win Standish and I have both thought, but unless you have some money—"

"I have none."

"Then they will take the place, and we had better think of what we can do, of where you can go."

"This is my place. It was given to your father by the *presidente* for your father's service in the Army of Mexico. I shall not see it taken from us."

"Señora, that president is dead. I do not know if the president we have now knows of our existence. Win and I have written and there has been no answer."

"As for the governor . . . Micheltorena is their friend, not ours. If it was Alvarado—"

"He is a man," Michael said.

"Agreed. But he is also a man out of office."

"Wooston will not stop with us. He is greedy. He will want more and more land."

"You know why he wants our land?"

"He is a smuggler. He wants to use Paradise Cove, as they used to, in the dark of night."

"It is not only that. He has heard stories about the gold."

Michael glanced at her. "If there is gold, why don't we get some of it now?"

She shrugged. "Only your father knew where it was. He was killed when he fell from his horse and had no chance to tell anyone."

"He must have said something, left some clue, some idea of where it came from?"

"No . . . nothing. All I know is that he would ride off and be gone for several days, in the desert, I think. He always rode out on a different route, but I do know that the place the gold came from was somewhere to the north. I say 'always' but he actually brought gold back on only two occasions."

"Why did he go then?"

"To explore. Your father was a soldier in the Army of Mexico for more than twenty years, and he had the gift of tongues. He could talk to almost any Indian we ever met, and he made friends everywhere.

"You know how it is here. Most of the Californios will not leave the missions or the pueblos. They like company and they are not adventurous. It was not so with Jaime. He loved the mountains and the desert, and was forever riding off to some lonely canyon or along some ancient trail he had found. I know how it was because I often went with him. But there is one clue."

"What?"

"When he went for the gold, he told of the trip, of the hard riding, the rough country . . . that sort of thing. But he always said 'we.' There was someone with him."

"Montero?"

"No, he always left Jesus here. Your father trusted him because Jesus was a sergeant in the old army when your father was a colonel. No, it had to be somebody we do not know."

"Look!" Michael got to his feet, indicating a dust cloud above the trail. "Someone is coming!"

"It's Win. Even when he is in a hurry your cousin rides like a soldier on parade."

Eileen Mulkerin put her hand on her son's shoulder. "You've been a good son, Michael, although sometimes I wish you had not become a monk. You were a fine hand with a rope or gun."

"Father was good. Very good."

She smiled. "He was that. And a fine upstanding man, too. I remember the first time I saw him. He was in uniform. He had a strong, bold way about him, and although he was half-Irish he looked the perfect hidalgo. He had just returned from campaigning against the Apache in Chihuahua, and I had come in on a ship from Ireland.

"There was a carriage to meet the ship and take me to my uncle's home. Jaime chanced to be there on some army business, and I was standing by the ship's rail."

"With all that red-gold hair?"

"Well? What was I to do with it? Pack it away in a trunk? Of course, I had it, and he saw it."

"He spoke of it once when we were riding. He said you were so beautiful he almost fell off his horse."

"He lied then. He never fell off a horse in his life, for any reason at all. Oh, we saw each other all right, and he came over, hat in hand, to help me into my carriage. He was the gallant one."

"Like Sean."

"Like both of you. There's a lot of him in you, Michael, and in Sean as well, and no better thing could be said of you."

Win Standish rode in, his horse dusty. He was a compact, solid young man of medium height, with a serious expression. He looked exactly like what he was, a rising young businessman.

"They are coming, Señora. I could not stop them. They would not listen and, of course, they have the law."

"Let them come."

Far down the road, the riders appeared. There were three of them.

"They'll get nothing. Nothing at all."

"There must be no violence now," Michael warned. "I cannot condone it."

"Nor I," Win added.

"Would you have me lose the place then?"

"You could not save it, Señora. They have the strength, and they have the law. You owe the money, and the debt is due."

"Yes, but we have the ranch, and we shall keep it. I lost a home in Ireland once, and I won't lose another."

The pace of the three riders slowed as they neared the ranch house. It was obvious that trouble was expected.

Zeke Wooston was a large, untidy man. Only a few years before he had come to California by the Panama route and had been involved in several doubtful business ventures. From the first he had curried favor with Captain Nick Bell, an adventurer who had been appointed commander of the local soldiery by Micheltorena. Micheltorena was a vacillating man who let his soldiers do as they wished, which to them meant robbing the citizens, drinking and carousing, and much random shooting. California was a long way from Mexico by ship or horseback, and not many soldiers wished that duty, so they had opened the prisons and the army that had come north to California was largely composed of confirmed criminals.

Jorge Fernandez, who rode with Wooston, was a lean, whiplash of a man known for his savage cruelty to horses, Indians, and women. Tomas Alexander owned a cantina on the road to Los Angeles. He was a gambler, smuggler, and bad man with a gun. It was said that he had many friends among the outlaws who hid in the canyons of the Santa Monica mountains.

Wooston started to dismount.

"No need to get down," Eileen Mulkerin said. "If you have business, state it."

"Señora, we have ridden far, if—"

"My door is open to friends and to strangers. You are neither."

"So that's how it is? All right, Señora, we'll make it plain. You pay up today or get out tomorrow. Go now and you may take your horses and personal belongings. Stay until tomorrow and you get nothing."

14

"We will pay."

"With what, Señora? With burned crops? With a few bales of hides? You have nothing, and nothing can come from nothing."

"The road lies there. Take it. You shall have your money."

Zeke Wooston leaned on the pommel. "Ma'am, we'll be back tomorrow with our men. If you ain't gone, we'll throw you off." His smile was not pleasant. "And ma'am, I won't care what happens to you when you get throwed off. I'll just leave you to my men."

"That rabble? You call those *men*?"

Turning their horses they rode back down the trail.

Win Standish watched them go, his expression indicating his worry. "Nothing is solved, Señora. You have only angered them."

"It gives us a little time, just a little more."

"Haven't you a clue about the gold?"

"It was Jaime's secret, and he died with it."

"I can talk to Pio," Win said after a minute, "but he is out of power and has troubles of his own. He and the governor do not see alike."

"Pio is only Pio. He is a good man, a very good man, and he is our friend, but at this moment our enemies have more strength."

Eileen Mulkerin looked toward the sea. From the porch only a narrow triangle of blue water could be seen, and it was empty. There would be gulls flying over that blue water, and driftwood on the beach. She loved to walk the damp sands when the tide first went out, as once she had walked it with Jaime, in their bare feet. She could no longer do that, for she was the Señora. Yet someday she would again.

"Sean will come," she said, at last. "He will find a way."

"If there was a way we would have found it," Win said, somewhat irritated. "I am afraid the place is lost."

Suddenly she could think of it no longer. Turning, she walked inside, fighting against the sudden rush of tears. How long since she had permitted herself to cry?

She stood for a minute, looking about, pressing her lips tightly together.

How bare the room was! How different from the rooms back in Ireland! Any furniture they had must be made on the spot or brought around the Horn by ship, which made it far too expensive.

There was a large table, a cowhide settee, two big chairs studded with brass nails, a handwoven rug on the floor, and a chest along the other wall. Over the mantel crossed halberds that Jaime had found up a canyon, souvenirs of some nameless battle lost by their owners.

Brother Michael followed her in. He sat down again, his loose brown robe giving no hint of the powerful muscles beneath. He had suddenly turned to religion after being known as a wild and somewhat dangerous young man. He never explained why, and nobody asked, respecting his privacy. When he wished to tell them, he would.

"We must think, Señora. There has to be some clue, some memory. You must take paper and pen and write down every memory you have. The writing will help to bring them to your mind, and among them there may be a clue, some little word, something he brought back . . . it might be anything."

Win Standish sat in one of the chairs. "Señora, I have thought of everything. You have many cattle, but so has everyone, and there is no market except for the hides. We have horses, but so has everyone. To sell the ranch would be impossible even if there was no loan against it. The last place that was sold brought only ten cents an acre . . . everyone has land."

"If it had not been for the fire," Brother Michael said, "all would have been well. I still think the Señora was right to plant wheat."

"And you had to borrow to buy the seed," Win agreed.

Eileen Mulkerin sighed. "That is past. What is done is done. The wheat was a good idea, and it was growing beautifully. We would have had the best income ever . . . and then the fire."

Brother Michael dismissed it with a gesture. "Twice father went to the mountains for gold and each time he found it. He must have known where he was going . . . the second time, at least."

"There was never very much. The first time was when you were born, Michael. Times were very bad, and we needed money. Your father took his horse and two others, one a pack horse."

"And a spare horse? For someone else to ride?"

"Who knows? Maybe to switch saddles and save the horse he rode."

"How much food? For a day? Three days? A week?"

"For a week, I think. It might have been more, but he would have hunted, too. He always killed game for meat."

"A week's ride?"

"If there was only something I could do!" Win said. "I've borrowed money on the store. I suppose I might—"

"You have done enough, more than enough."

She looked out over the hard-packed dooryard. Money was hard to come by in California in 1844. There was food, good beef, beans, all the necessities,

17

but cash was another thing. It seemed that everybody was in the same situation, and now this.

She remembered how they had first come to the mountains of Malibu, to this quiet place in the hills. The hills were brown then, so unlike the hills of her beloved Ireland, and more like those of Spain.

After they had fled Ireland they had gone to France on a smuggler's boat, and she had lived there for a few months, and then her father had gone to Spain and sent for his family to follow.

He had been involved in a plot to rebel against the British government and it had been discovered. A friendly Englishman who liked her father had warned him and he had fled. After her father had died in Spain she had come to Mexico to live with an aunt and uncle. It was then that she met Jaime.

She had fallen in love with the lonely beaches, with the occasional sea lions on the sand, even with the huge bears they saw from time to time back in the hills.

Colonel Mulkerin had always enjoyed hunting, and she had gone with him many times. He hunted only for meat, but few of the Californios hunted at all, and even fewer went into the mountains.

On those forays into the hills they often met Indians, and sometimes they met them on the beach. Most of them were the Chumash, a bright, intelligent lot whose plank boats, painted red, often carried as many as twenty people on voyages back and forth to the offshore islands. Their name was not really Chumash, but the first of their tribe to become acquainted with the white man were from a group inhabiting San Miguel Island and their name was Chumash, so the name was applied to all of them.

Eileen Mulkerin walked across to the other chair and sat down. "It was what we wanted," she said after awhile. "This was just what we wanted but we did not know until we saw it."

The cottonwood leaves rustled in the wind, and she looked out the door at the blue water, so far away. "Until we left Ireland the largest cities I had seen were Dublin and Cork, but after that there was Paris, Marseilles, Madrid, Cordova, and finally Mexico City. When I married Jaime and the *presidente* gave him this grant to come north, we both knew it was home."

"We liked the Indians. They were very quiet and reserved, but when we spoke they always replied. One day we were driving to the pueblo in a cart and we came upon a group walking to the tar pits. We invited them to ride and told them we would take them back with the tar they used to seal the seams of their boats.

"After that we were friends. Often they brought us fish, and just as often, Jaime gave them venison. It was on one of the trips to their camp on the shore with venison that we met Juan."

"Juan?" Michael frowned. "I don't remember him."

"It was before you were born. We took the Indians meat and talked to them as they cooked it, but one man sat off by himself, staring at the sea. I asked who he was. 'He is of another people,' the Indians said.

"His nose was thinner, his skin a bit lighter, his eyes larger, but he was old, very, very old."

"Another tribe?" Michael asked.

"Another people. But he was their friend. We started to ride away, knowing no more about him. He was walking back from the beach. Jaime pulled up and spoke to him. 'You seem alone. Come to visit us whenever you wish.'"

"He replied, surprisingly, in English. 'I will.'"

"Jaime waved at the hills, the far, unknown hills. 'Perhaps you know about them. I would like to know the trails, the people, the villages, especially the places where no men go. It is a beautiful land.' The old man listened, then walked on without speaking. Two weeks later he was sitting on the beach one morning when we came by."

Chapter 2

Captain Sean Mulkerin, of the two-masted schooner *Lady Luck* stood on the afterdeck staring at the scattered lights of the sleepy village of Acapulco. It was a straggling town of some three thousand people against an exciting backdrop of mountains and forest.

Tomorrow, at daylight, they would sail for home, and Sean Mulkerin was for once unhappy at the prospect. He had sailed south with too small a cargo and its sale had not gone well. Hides were a drug on the market and he had gotten rid of them for only a dollar and a half each instead of the expected two dollars.

They had done better with their furs, especially the otter pelts, but they would be lucky even to show a profit after expenses were deducted. He had hoped to bring home enough to pay off the loan on the ranch.

Owing to the depths of the harbor, a vessel could lie close in off the sandy beach, so the lights of the town were near. A few scattered houses and two cantinas still showed light, and there was another light at the Spanish fort that once guarded the harbor.

Two more vessels lay at anchor, one a ship newly arrived from Manila, the other a schooner, three-masted and considerably larger than the *Lady Luck*.

The night was hot and still with a feeling of impending change in the weather. Leaning on the rail he looked shoreward, an undefined longing inside him, a yearning for something that lay over there, something for him.

He had always felt this way in seaport towns, always looked at the lights reflecting upon the dark water and wondered who awaited him there, what loves, what adventures, what dreams . . . or perhaps death and a bloody dagger. A man never knew, and that was the thing. A man never knew.

Whichever way he turned there might be some haunting mystery, some enchantment. This way might lie love and fortune, and that way shame and death.

He straightened up, stretched, and turned away. He was starting for his cabin when a movement caught his attention.

Someone was running across the sand toward the water . . . it looked like . . . it was . . . a woman. As she reached the water's edge she threw off her outer garment and plunged into the sea, swimming strongly.

Startled, he turned back to the rail, but could see nothing on the dark water. Once he thought he saw the flash of a white arm, and then ashore a door slammed and someone called out.

There was a shouted question, a reply, then a babble of excited yells, with men rushing back and forth.

Suddenly there was a faint splash right under the taffrail and a low voice called up to him. "Unless you wish me to drown, throw me a rope."

It was a woman's voice, and for an instant he was startled into stillness. Then he turned swiftly to the rope ladder that hung over the side amidships and shook it against the hull so she would hear. "This way!" he called softly, and she swam along the hull to the ladder.

She caught hold, began to climb clumsily, and a moment later he helped her over the rail. She shook her long hair, then started to wring the water from it. Her dress had been left behind and she stood in a soaking chemise and pantalets.

"Don't stand there staring!" she said impatiently. "Get me a coat, or something, and then you'd better get away from here."

"We aren't sailing until morning," Sean said, still stunned by the rapid movement of events.

"Take my advice and go now or you'll find yourself in jail. My being here will take a lot of explaining." She nodded toward the shore. "That pack of fools will find my dress and they will search every ship in the harbor."

"That's all I'd need!" he said, and turning sharply he called down the companionway. "Ten! Pedro! Congo! On deck!"

Ten Tennison was first on deck.

"Get the anchor in and enough canvas to move her. No lights. I want to move out as quietly as possible."

He ran forward and shook out the jib and by the time he reached the fo'c's'le two men were beside him and the schooner was already moving.

Tennison had taken the wheel. "Keep her stern to the town. The longer it takes them to realize we're moving, the better."

Pedro was sharp and quick and not the kind to waste time with questions. He could hear the tumult and shouting ashore and had no wish to be caught up in what was happening.

The breeze was slight, but the schooner was an easy sailer and took the wind nicely, gliding smoothly through the water. From the shore no perceptible movement could be seen unless someone watched the mastheads against a star.

"La Boca Chica," Sean said, indicating the smaller of the two entrances.

The girl had disappeared and he was just as pleased, for he had no wish to answer the crew's questions now. He swore softly, bitterly. The last thing they needed now was to have the schooner seized and her crew in prison.

Creating scarcely a ripple, the schooner slid through the three-hundred-yard gap between Point Pilar and Point Grifo and into the sea.

Outside there was a good bit of breeze. "Get everything we've got on her, Ten. We've got to run for it."

When the canvas was aloft Ten came aft. "Thought you weren't sailing until daybreak?" he said, quizzically.

With as few words as possible, Sean explained. Tennison was his mate, a fine sailorman who had begun his life on the coast of Maine, had fished the Grand Banks until he longed for broader, warmer seas, and had sailed out to China on the big tea ships.

"Who is she? Some jailbird?"

"Looks and talks like a lady, but I wouldn't know. I just wish I'd never seen her and she hadn't seen our schooner!"

The wind filled the sails, and the *Lady Luck* dipped her bows deeper, then rode up out of the water like the dainty ship she was, shaking the water from her. The wind was fair and she laid over a bit.

She was an easy craft to handle, and a fast one. Nothing on the coast could touch her unless it was that new schooner. It had more canvas.

"Keep her west by northwest, Ten. I'll go below and see if I can find out what this is all about."

He went down the companionway to the small cabin. She had crawled into a bunk, his bunk, and was fast asleep. Her wet clothing lay on the deck.

He stared at her and swore under his breath. Of all the damned fool . . . she was pretty, though. Too damned pretty!

No wonder they had chased her.

He turned the light low and returned to the deck. Tennison grinned at him. "You didn't stay long."

"She's asleep. What could I do, Ten? She swam out to the schooner and came up the ladder. They were hunting her ashore, and they'd never believe we weren't involved somehow."

"You done right. You'd no choice."

"She's got no wedding ring on her finger. I saw that much."

He walked forward, trying to think the situation through. He could find no alternative to what he had done. Of course, he could immediately have called ashore and let them come and take her, which would have been neither gallant nor right. She was obviously not a thief. At least, he smiled wryly, dressed as she was she could not have carried much with her.

He had no choice but to do as he had done. But, what if this brought more trouble to his family? If there was some place he could take her—.

There was no place.

The sea was picking up and *Lady Luck* was making good time. California was a long way from Acapulco, and even if they guessed that she had some aboard the *Lady Luck* there was small chance of them chasing her all that distance.

He had not planned to sail until daybreak, but who knew that? And he had no connection with her nor she with him, so it might be some time before anyone tied them together.

He walked aft again. "You'd better turn in," Tennison said. "Use my bunk."

He *was* tired. At four o'clock he must take over the watch from Tennison. Sean Mulkerin went below and dropped on Tennison's bunk. He was asleep almost at once.

At four when he came on deck there was a strong sea running but the *Lady* was taking it gracefully, as always. The sky was overcast and the deck was wet from a recent shower.

Congo was at the wheel and Tennison was standing in the stern, looking back at the horizon.

"See anything?"

Tennison shrugged. "Thought I glimpsed a masthead back there but I was probably mistaken. Even so it might have been some ship headed up the Gulf for Mazatlán."

It was not yet light although the sky was gray along the eastern horizon. With a glance at the canvas, all taut and shipshape, Sean walked to the wheel and glanced at the compass.

The run from Acapulco to Paradise Cove was something over fifteen hundred miles, two to three weeks sailing if all went well. If the wind held it could be somewhat less, but the sea had a way of making its own rules. Wind and wave could be understood but not predicted beyond a point. There was always the unexpected calm or the unexpected storm.

It was daylight when he took the wheel and he was still there when the girl came on deck.

She had contrived a dress from his serape and some pins, and looked incredibly lovely. Her skin was clear and olive-toned, and her hair black.

"I am Mariana de la Cruz," she said, "and I wish to thank you."

"I am Sean Mulkerin."

"You are the captain? And Irish?"

"Yes. My mother is Irish, my father was Irish and Mexican."

"Was?"

"He was killed about a year ago."

"Have you seen anything?" Her eyes searched his. "I mean is anyone following us?"

"I doubt it. Were you expecting to be followed?"

She thought for a moment, her eyes wide and dark. Then she nodded, "Yes, I believe he will follow. Andres is a very determined man, and not at all a forgiving one."

"Andres?"

"Andres Machado. I was to have married him today."

Andres Machado! It would have to be him, of all people. A man fiercely proud, and a noted duelist and fighting man. Yes, he would certainly follow. Whether he wanted this girl or not he would never allow her to leave him.

"It was not my choice . . . the marriage, I mean. My father is dead, and Andres arranged it with my uncle. I refused him once, and he did not like that.

"We were to be married in Acapulco. Andres' aunt and her maid were with us, and my uncle was to come down from our ranch. I hate Andres and I could not bear the thought of marrying him. Then I saw you in the plaza. Somebody mentioned who you were, and that you were going to be sailing back to California.

"When the maid turned down my bed, she left and I did not think she would be back. It was the only chance I had to escape so I ran out . . . and then she came back, probably to spy on me."

Sean glanced at the compass and moved the wheel a spoke, scowling thoughtfully. He knew a good deal about Machado, and had even been friendly with him at one time. Their friendship ended abruptly when he had beaten Machado in a horse race, but he knew Machado well.

Andres came from a good family, but he was a spoiled and arrogant young man who would not be frustrated in anything and who could not accept defeat.

Would he follow them? Of course he would. No doubt about it, and doubly so since he, Sean Mulkerin, was the one involved. Machado would never believe that he had not known Mariana de la Cruz before, that this had not been contrived to make him look ridiculous.

The worst of it was that Machado could afford his whims, for he was as wealthy as he was politically powerful.

This was trouble, serious trouble, and at such a time when his family needed no more trouble than it already had.

Sean glanced astern. The horizon was clear, but at this height above the sea the visibility was only a few miles. People unaccustomed to the sea always imagined they could see very far indeed, but the distance to the horizon was simply calculated. One took the square root of the eye above the sea, multiplied it by 1.15 and had the approximate distance. If the height of the eye above the sea was nine feet one could see about three and one-half miles.

"Hilo," he shouted to one of the men suddenly, "run aloft and take a look astern."

Hilo, a Hawaiian, scrambled aloft, hesitated only a moment, then called, "A schooner, sir! Ten or twelve miles off!"

"A two-master?"

"Three, sir."

"Thanks, Hilo." He glanced at the sea ahead, calculating their chances. Machado had wasted no time. He swore to himself. Then, recalling that Mariana was standing there, he said, "Oh, I beg your pardon!"

"Captain, do not apologize. I am sorry. I had no idea—"

"No, you didn't," he agreed bluntly. "That schooner is undoubtedly the one that lay at anchor in the harbor at Acapulco, and she looked like a good sailer."

"I have gotten you into trouble!" she said.

"I do not mind trouble," he said, "but at this time trouble for me is trouble for my family. This schooner may soon be all we have. Nothing must happen to it."

If his family were not waiting for him, he would have been tempted to run west for Hawaii, to lose them at sea. He knew many a trick, and if time was no object—

"I am sorry," Mariana repeated.

"What's done is done. Now we must see how we can get out of it."

"Machado is a good friend to Micheltorena, the governor of California."

"He would be." Sean was in no mood for politeness. "Have you any more tidbits like that?"

"Only that he is no friend to Pio Pico or Alvarado."

"They are friends of my mother and were friends of my father, but that does us no good now. Neither has the power of Micheltorena, nor of Machado, for that matter."

He put the wheel over a few spokes, glancing at the sails. He would head more westerly, try to edge away from the sailing routes to San Diego and points north. He would head for the open sea.

All day long they scudded over the sea, a gray-green sea studded with whitecaps. Several times he sent a man aloft and at the last report the other schooner was still headed northwest. If they had been seen, the big schooner was not responding.

At supper in the cabin he sat alone with Mariana and put his worries aside. He talked quietly of California, of his brother and his mother, and of Los Angeles, the tiny pueblo toward which they were sailing. He spoke mostly of the Señora. "She rules us," he said, smiling a little, "and she is usually right. But you will like her and you can stay with us as long as we have a roof over our heads." He grinned wryly. "Which may not be long."

"Hadn't you better think about that? You'll have more time for thinking now than when we're ashore."

At midnight he returned to the deck, took a sighting on a star, then turned in. Tennison sent Congo for him at four in the morning.

Tennison returned to the deck after breakfast and the sea was empty. From the masthead they could see nothing.

Chapter 3

From the starboard bow Captain Sean Mulkerin looked toward the California coast which lay just over the horizon. The big schooner would be over there, beating up the coast, perhaps sailing a little slower to check the coves for hiding places.

Sean knew he was postponing the inevitable. Machado was a shrewd man, and he might sail right on to San Pedro and make contact with the authorities in Los Angeles.

A cold wind was blowing on this morning, and the sea was choppy.

At twenty-two Sean Mulkerin was a veteran of several years at sea. Born on the ranch at Malibu he had grown up herding cattle, hunting and wandering in the mountains, breaking wild horses, and sailing to the Channel Islands with the Chumash.

At fourteen he made his first voyage with his father. They sailed down the coast to Mazatlán, Acapulco, and Tehuantepec. His second voyage, later the same year, was to Panama, Callao, and Valparaiso. Another six months ashore and he was back at sea again, now grown to his full height of five feet and ten inches. This voyage took him to Hawaii, Shanghai, Macao, and Taku Bar. The ship had started for home when it reached Taku Bar and word of rich cargoes in the Moluccas turned them back. From there they had sailed to Samoa and Tahiti before returning home.

At sixteen Sean weighed one hundred and eighty pounds. Between the hard work on the ranch and at sea he had grown tough and strong. And at eighteen made his first trip as mate. By that time he was a veteran of dozens of brawls in as many ports.

The frequent wars and rebellions in Latin America had spawned a number of privateers sailing under letters of marque from one country or another, most of them with European crews prepared to attack any likely looking ship, whether an enemy vessel or not.

The *Lady Luck*, like many another merchant vessel of the time, was armed. She carried four guns amidships and a Long Tom on the stern.

Sean's first sea fight had occurred on his first voyage, an hour-long battle with a privateer in the Gulf of Tehuantepec. *Lady Luck*'s amidship guns were below deck, concealed behind ports invisible from more than a hundred and fifty feet. The privateer, a brig with sixteen guns anticipated no trouble. Ordering *Lady Luck* to heave to, it closed in rapidly.

30

Jaime Mulkerin had been master of his own ship on that voyage. He was sure that he could outrun the brig but he needed sea room.

Expecting no trouble, the privateers had not manned their guns. They could see the Long Tom astern but no gunner was near it and unless the schooner changed course that gun could not be brought to bear.

"Load with canister," Jaime ordered. "Fire at my word and try to sweep their decks. Reload immediately and aim at their water line." He stood at the wheel.

His crew was six men, and at least forty privateers could be seen on the brig. Slowly the brig drew abreast, and at thirty yards range, Jaime gave the order. The ports flew up, the guns ran out.

From the brig there was a shout of alarm, drowned in the boom of *Lady Luck*'s two starboard guns. The unexpected blast of fire swept the deck of the other ship.

Caught by surprise the brig had no chance to man her guns. The decks were bloody, littered with the dead and dying, and her one shot had whistled harmlessly between the schooner's two masts.

The Long Tom, loaded with solid shot, struck the mainmast, ripped a chunk from it and passed on through the afterdeckhouse. Jaime Mulkerin shook out all of his ship's canvas and the *Lady Luck* began to pull away. Standing in the stern Jaime gave a parting wave of his cap.

It was his mother who worried Sean now. The Señora was a strong, capable woman, even more so since the death of her husband, and her present difficulty was due more to bad luck than to mismanagement. Some of that bad luck might have been arranged by those who wanted the ranch.

There had always been fires along the California

coast. The chaparral that cloaked the hills of the south-ern coast was a thick growth of evergreen shrubs that grew from three to twelve feet tall, with small, stiff leaves and crooked branches closely intertwined to form an almost impenetrable thicket. There was also a variety of scrub oak, manzanita, chamisal, yucca, and mountain mahogany, all highly inflammable. In the hot, dry months of late summer and fall it was a dangerous combination.

Yet scattered among these chaparral-covered hills there were occasional canyons with running streams, their shores lined with valley sycamore, cottonwood, willow and other trees. There were also lovely green meadows, excellent for farming or grazing. The Señora had planted some of these meadows with wheat and corn. Her crops were growing spendidly when the fires came, wiping them out. The fires might have been accidental, or they might not.

Sean wondered if there could be a way out. For him, of course, there was the schooner. For his brother there was the Church. But what about the Señora? Since his father's death the ranch had become her life, perhaps all that was left of her life. At all costs, the Malibu must not be lost.

Tennison came forward. "Cap'n? How do we go in?"

Sean thought for a moment, although his mind had been made up hours ago. He just wanted to review his plan before acting upon it.

"We'll go inside San Nicolas Island," he said, "and outside of Santa Barbara Island. When we come around Santa Barbara we'll head right for the coast. I want to drop anchor off the kelp and get the canvas off her at once."

"At night?"

"If it works out that way, and I believe it will. If

the weather holds we can make it easily, and we'll just lie up behind Santa Barbara until dark. No lights after that."

When Mariana came on deck the sky was gray and overcast, the sea choppy with a few whitecaps. "What will your mother think of me?" she asked suddenly.

"She will love you."

"How can she? When I bring you only trouble?"

He shrugged. "There is always trouble. One learns to live with it. A man grows through enduring."

"Is that why you go to sea?"

He chuckled. "Of course not. I go to sea because it is a means to a living. Nobody in his right mind invites difficulties, you simply cope with those that do arise. But you don't try to avoid your duties. As far as the sea is concerned, you learn to live *with* the sea or you don't last. You simply try to conform."

"What about people? Do you conform there, too?"

"Whenever I can, of course. Why not? Most rules whether of law or good breeding are simply made to enable men to live together with less friction. If one lives with people he must always conform, to a degree. I see no harm in that, and lose nothing by it."

He paused, staring off to sea. San Nicolas Island was ahead and somewhat to the west. He looked at it a moment, studying it thoughtfully. These outer islands had a pattern, and if one learned about them, navigation in the channels was much simpler. The Chumash had told him that the slightest change in color could mean a change of wind, often of current.

Yet he was scarcely thinking of them as he looked, for he was thinking of Mariana.

For two weeks they had eaten every meal together, had stood watches together, walked the decks together. Was he falling in love? That was ridiculous, and yet—

The *Lady Luck* was an honest ship, answering easily to the helm and carrying her canvas well.

It had never ceased to amaze him how men with good tools were able to shape timber and create something as splendid as a ship. And how a ship, once built, could take on a life and character of its own. How it leaves the land behind, gives itself to the sea, and how the rough timbers become translated into a kind of poetry.

Sean said as much to Mariana, and she listened more to the man than to the words. He felt it and was disturbed. He was not quite sure what was the right thing, and he wanted to do the right thing. His years at sea had not made him a cynic, nor had they hardened him, and he knew what proximity on shipboard could do to people and how quickly it could disappear once they were on the beach again.

"We'll be going in," he said, "as soon as it is dark."

"Isn't that dangerous?"

"Not for us. We've sailed this coast many times, and I'd rather they not see us until we've met and talked to my family. I want them to have a chance to meet you and understand what has happened." He hesitated for a moment. "We may have to leave then. Have you any friends up this way? Any relatives?"

"No."

He hunched his shoulders inside his coat, staring at the rough shoulder of Santa Barbara Island.

"Why not let me take you back to your uncle?"

She turned to stare at him. "Do you want me to go back?"

Uncomfortably, he avoided her eyes. "No. Whatever is best for you."

"If I went back to him he would simply hold me for Andres. They made an arrangement."

He turned away from the subject, thinking about what Machado might do. Would he sail up the coast? More likely, he would come overland to the ranch, and that could mean a fight.

What was Sean doing to the Señora, anyway?

Maybe they should run for it, up the coast to Monterey, and go to Alvarado. He was no longer in power but he had influence, and even the governor would hesitate to invite trouble with him.

The schooner moved out from behind the island, caught the wind, and began a run for the coast. Behind them the sun declined, the peaks on the island took on a reddish glow, and the sea grew darker.

When Tennison came on deck to relieve him Sean said, "Nothing in sight, but keep an eye open for Indians, some of them may be running in for the coast now."

"Cap'n?" he said suddenly. "I've put by a few dollars. If the Señora—"

"Thanks, Ten. We'll make out. We need a big chunk, several thousand dollars, and that kind of money is scarce on this coast."

"Don't you be takin' that Machado lightly," Ten said. "He's killed a half-dozen men in duels, and some of them for little or nothing."

"Hold her steady, Ten. If the wind holds we should be up to the kelp by midnight or a little after. I'll be up to take her in."

The coast lay dark along the horizon now, the Santa Monicas a serrated blackness against the sky and the stars. It was warm and still in the cabin, the brass lamp turned low, swinging gently with the movement of the schooner.

"Tomorrow," he said softly, "tomorrow we'll be home, and I hope all's well."

Chapter 4

It was completely dark when Sean returned to the deck. He closed the door behind him so that no light would show, and the schooner's lights had been extinguished. They were moving slower now under a jib and fo'c's'le.

There was a light breeze, and the clouds were broken, allowing a glimpse of stars from time to time. Before them the shore was a black, ominous wall.

"We're coming up to the kelp," Tennison said. "The point is yonder."

A light appeared suddenly atop a ridge back of the point. "There it is," Tennison muttered. "Your man never misses."

"I hope he never does," Sean replied, "but tonight we could take her in, anyway."

The light atop the ridge, as both Tennison and Sean knew, was actually in a niche in the rocks that could not be seen except from the sea, and at that only from certain angles.

Taking the wheel Sean guided the *Lady Luck* along the edge of the kelp. The cove was about two miles northeast of the point. There was a reef to be avoided just south of the point, and a breaking rock closer in. Where he wanted to anchor was just outside the kelp with a sand bottom at about seven fathoms.

They moved on slowly, and after a few minutes Sean said, "All right, Ten, let go the anchor."

He listened to the anchor running out, timing the chain as it ran through the hawsehole. The crew were furling the sails, and soon the schooner lay under bare poles, her dark green hull lost against the kelp and the shoreline.

Tennison came aft again. "Dinghy's over, Cap'n. You want we should stand by?"

"Do that. If anything develops while I am gone, use your own judgment. If they come after you by boat, take 'em through the kelp. You know where it can be done and they do not."

Congo had dropped a rope ladder over the side. "Your rifle, sah," Congo's voice was soft for such a big man, carrying the warmth of the West Indies in its tone. "I thought you might be needing it, sah."

"Thanks, Congo."

Mariana came on deck, wrapped in her serape.

Sean Mulkerin went over swiftly, almost dropping into the bobbing boat. He held the ladder while Mariana came down, showing some caution but no hesitation. She was a girl, he decided, about whom there was very little nonsense, and she could act as swiftly on occasion as he himself.

Congo followed, and sat at the oars. He pushed off into the darkness.

The water was black, with only a few ripples from the kelp. They could hear the rustling of the surf on the sand. Congo used the oars only to give direction. There was just enough sea running to carry them in.

It was very dark and still. Looking up, Mariana saw one lone star peeping through a rift in the clouds. Congo pulled strongly and she felt the bow grate on the sand. Sean leaped over and pulled the boat higher, then extended a hand to help her ashore.

"Go back, Congo, and thanks."

The big black man shoved the boat into the water, then stepped in. "Cap'n, if you want, I can sure come back. If there's fightin' to do—?"

"You'd be the first I'd call," Sean said, "and thanks again. Take care of the *Lady Luck* for me."

A cool wind blew along the sand and they stood together watching the boat, listening to the *chunk* of the oars in the oarlocks.

They walked along the dark beach, pausing from time to time to listen. Sean was wary. He could have chosen to anchor in Dume Cove, which was closer to the ranch house, but if Machado was already searching for them, that was where they would look to find the schooner.

"Is it far?" she asked after a minute.

"A few minutes, that is all. You will rest well tonight and the Señora will find some proper clothes for you."

"She will hate me. I bring you trouble."

"She will love you." He hesitated. "Mariana, one thing you should know, and which you will see soon enough. My mother is a very beautiful woman."

"But of course—!"

"I do not mean she is beautiful because she is my mother, she is simply beautiful . . . and very Irish. She will love you, but she is strong-minded, perfectly capable of holding her own with anyone."

"How does such a strong woman have a strong son? Often it is otherwise."

"We had a strong father, but they never opposed each other, they worked as a team. It was a revelation to many people."

The cart was there, with one horse. It took shape from the darkness, and then they saw Jesus Montero sitting on the sand close by, a rifle across his knees.

"*Buenos noches, señor . . . señorita.*"

She could make out little in the darkness except that the man was old.

To Sean he said, "There is much trouble, señor. They came to take the ranch, and they will come again tomorrow."

"Who came?"

"Señor Wooston, the big one. Fernandez was with him, and Tomas Alexander."

"A pack of thieves."

"There was another one, señor. A man called Russell."

"Ah?"

King-Pin Russell, renegade, free-booter, and all-around bad man. A man who would do anything, stop at nothing.

"How did Wooston get into this?"

"I know only what I hear. I believe he bought debts from others, threatened them in some cases. I heard from my people that he went to people from whom you had borrowed. Some did not know he was a bad man. Valdez did not. With some he threatened force."

"That sounds like Wooston . . . and Russell."

"Señora waits for you. She has confidence."

Sean felt a pang. She was expecting help from him and he had brought her only trouble. Yet there had to be something . . . some way. . . .

On a brush-covered knoll, overlooking the trail up the canyon, Tomas Alexander waited with Russell.

"I tell you, Tomas, this here's no good. He ain't comin'."

"There was a rider. A man who comes from the port to the pueblo. He said a big schooner had come in and Mulkerin left ahead of them, so he should be here."

"We looked in the cove. There was nothin'."

"He is a shrewd one, Sean Mulkerin is. He knows this coast and might anchor elsewhere. Anyway," Tomas shrugged, "he might not come in until after dark."

Russell took a pull at his bottle and put it aside.

Sitting out in these dark hills was not what he considered a good time. He dug out more of a hollow for his hip and then settled down to sleep. Yet it seemed he had scarcely closed his eyes when Tomas spoke.

"They come, amigo. I hear a cart."

Russell eased himself forward to a selected firing position. Wooston had said to kill Mulkerin, and that was just what he intended to do.

He peered along the rifle barrel, then stopped. "There's three of them!" he said exasperatedly. "How do we know which is him?"

"He won't be driving, and he has very broad shoulders."

Russell could see the three figures taking shape, suddenly he heard low laughter. "Hell," he said, "there's a woman with him!"

"Careful, amigo," Tomas warned, "if it is a woman it is a lady. He would bring no woman to his mother unless she was a lady."

Russell had been lifting his rifle to fire, but now he hesitated. One could be sure of killing one, and with a bit of luck, two. But the third one? There was too much risk that one would get away, and people who live talk. He relaxed slowly.

"A lady? Who would that be?"

"I do not know, but we must be careful, amigo. They know many important people. The Señora has many good friends, and it could be the wife or daughter of some important man. If you shoot, she might be hurt."

Russell waited, then withdrew his rifle. He was just as pleased, for he did not like the odds. Suppose he killed the woman? That could be a hanging offense, and if it was somebody important he would get no help from Wooston. Zeke did not like mistakes.

Also, he had no wish to have a live Sean Mulkerin

hunting the chaparral for him. Undoubtedly Mulkerin knew this area better than he ever would, and a man had little choice of trails. You couldn't push through chaparral very easily, it was all so tightly woven together, and in any case, it would be noisy. Usually you had to stick to trails, and Sean Mulkerin had grown up here.

"Let's get out of here."

Tomas hesitated, wanting to go yet not liking the prospect of facing Wooston, a man he feared. Finally he said, "To my cantina. We will have a bottle of wine and talk of this. Maybe there is another way."

Working their way back down the path, they reached their horses.

Eileen Mulkerin had been awakened by a voice outside her window. It was Montero's voice and she had been expecting it.

"They are here, Señora," he said, speaking softly. "They come from the sea."

"*Gracias*, Jesus."

She lay still for a moment, thinking of her son. He had sailed away with very little, and the market for pelts and hides was always uncertain. She did not expect him to return to her with enough money to pay off what was owed. That was impossible.

But just that he be here, to stand beside her, to help her face what was coming.

"Jaime," she said softly, but aloud. "Jaime, I need you."

Sean was like him in so many ways, yet was his own man. She thought again of this son of hers, who each time he returned from the sea seemed somehow older, wiser, more sure of himself, yet different, too.

That was what experience did to a man, experience

and time. Sean had always been slow to express opinions, careful in his judgments, and the sea had done that for him also. The sea demands consideration always, no man upon the deep water may make decisions without careful consideration of wind and wave. She remembered Sean telling her how the Polynesians could tell when an island lay over the horizon and out of sight by the currents or the condition of the water.

She dressed quickly and went into the kitchen. Always at such times her first thought was of food and a warm drink for the traveler.

She made coffee from their small stock. Sean liked coffee but they could buy it rarely. Tea was the more common drink. The Indians often drank a tea made from ephedra, which she had come to like.

She warmed a stew Carlotta had made earlier that day. Coming in at *night?* Why? It was unlike Sean, for as well as he knew the California coast he was a careful seaman, never taking unnecessary risks.

Worried now, she went outside and stood in the chill of the night. California was a semidesert land and the desert cools off quickly at night. There was a breeze in from the sea, and she stood there, listening.

Somewhere a mockingbird was singing his endless songs, frogs were croaking down by the little creek, but their sounds only emphasized the stillness.

As the cart slowly emerged from the darkness, she saw three people on the seat.

Jesus was there, and Sean, and a girl.

A very beautiful girl.

Chapter 5

Sean got down, then helped the girl down. They turned toward the porch. Sean hugged his mother but before he could speak the girl stepped forward a little.

"Señora? I am Mariana de la Cruz, and I am afraid I have brought you trouble."

"Trouble? Very pretty trouble then. Will you come in?" Eileen Mulkerin turned to the door, pausing only to say, "Thank you, Jesus. *Gracias.*"

"*Por nada, Señora.*"

"There's coffee. Will you be seated? Riding that cart up from the ocean at night is not . . . well, perhaps it is not the best welcome we could offer."

Sean started to speak, but Mariana stopped him. "Let me explain, Señora. I was in trouble. I was being forced to marry a man I did not love, whom I did not wish to marry, and I saw your son and I saw his ship.

"I needed help desperately, and he had a strong, kind face, so when night came I slipped away and swam to his schooner."

"Very romantic," Eileen said, dryly. "And what will your betrothed say to this?"

"He followed us," Sean replied. "He is Andres Machado. I am afraid I have brought you trouble, Señora, when there is trouble enough."

"Andres Machado." The Señora smiled a little grimly. "When you decide to make enemies, Sean, you do not pick them easy."

"It was my fault," Mariana said.

Eileen glanced at her, irritated at the new trouble but liking the proud, strong look in the girl's face. "It was your fault, and my son could have and would have done nothing else, but we have had troubles before and will have them again. You are welcome here."

"If you wish, I can go away. I can find friends. My father had friends in California."

"You may stay here, and welcome. As for your friends, you may need them. I know a great deal about Andres Machado."

Over coffee, they talked of what lay before them, and after a while Sean said, "Is Michael here?"

"He is."

"Then he will have to stay. I do not think they would dare to forcibly eject a man of the Church."

"And what do you expect me to do?" she demanded.

"We must think of that, Señora. This is your ranch. You are in command here. However, we must never yield possession. I know Michael, and he is immovable. If he says he will stay, he will stay.

"As for us, it might be better to disappear, to keep out of sight so they cannot serve you with papers."

"That does nothing but delay them."

Suddenly Win Standish appeared in the door, Michael behind him. "We heard voices," Win said. "How are you, Sean? A good voyage?"

"Only the weather. The hides went for a dollar and fifty cents. We did somewhat better on the pelts."

"You paid expenses?"

"No more than that."

Turning, Sean presented Mariana. His explanation was brief.

Win's face stiffened. "The last thing we want is trouble with Andres Machado. He is a rich, powerful, and vindictive man. If you think we have trouble with Wooston, it will be nothing to what Machado can do."

"We must return her to them," Win said. "She was betrothed to Machado. It was her father's wish."

"I will not marry him! I will die first!"

"It was your father's wish," Brother Michael replied gently. "Do you not respect your parents?"

44

"My father was not concerned. My father is dead. This is my uncle who wishes to be rid of me, and of Andres, who wants a wife for his home."

"She should have something to say about whom she marries," Sean said quietly.

"We cannot afford this trouble," Standish interrupted. "And if we lose the ranch, where will she go then?"

"One thing at a time," Sean said.

"You are all forgetting the ranch," Eileen said. "It is the first consideration."

"It has been a bad year," Win Standish said, "and I have given all I can."

"It has been much, more than enough. You have been loyal, Win." Eileen spoke quietly. "It was more than we had a right to expect of you."

Jesus Montero sat in a corner twisting his hat in his hands. "There is the old man," he said, "Juan. He went with Don Jaime to the mountains."

"You mean," Win turned on him, "when the colonel found the gold?"

"It was not much gold," Montero said, "only a little bit. However, it was enough."

"I have never believed in the gold," Standish said. "Nobody has found gold in California."

"That is not true," Sean replied. "There was a vaquero who found some in one of the canyons. It was a few nuggets clinging to the roots of a wild onion. There is gold."

"Stories!" Win scoffed. "Just stories!"

"Do you know the mountains, Montero?" Eileen asked.

"Who knows them? Nobody. Not even the Indians know them. When you ride into them and think you know them you come back later and they have changed. My people do not go to the mountains, Señora."

"But you do know where the old man is?"

Montero shrugged. "Perhaps. Who can say? He comes and he goes and if he does not wish you to see him you do not see him. I have not seen him since a year before Don Jaime died. He may be dead now . . . or gone."

"Gone?"

"They disappear sometimes, the old ones do. They disappear and one finds nothing, nothing at all. Who knows where they go? One day they are here, and the next they are gone."

"The old man, Montero? Can you take me to him?" Sean asked.

"I can try. If he is alive and wishes to be found, we will find him. If he does not wish it, we will not."

"What kind of Indian is he?" Michael asked.

Montero shrugged. "Who knows? Some say he was one of those who named the land, those who were here before the Chumash and are gone now.

"Who knows what Malibu means? Latecomers have tried to say it means where the mountains meet the sea, but it is not true. Nobody knows . . . nor Mugu . . . nor Hueneme. The names were given long ago to the land, and the people who gave them are gone. All but this old man."

"Have you seen him, Sean?" Michael asked.

"Twice . . . once when I was only a small boy I met him near Sandstone Peak. He talked to me . . . for a long time."

"You never told me of that," Eileen protested. "What did he say?"

"It was something he was teaching me. A lot of words. He got up and left very suddenly, but before he left me he stopped to say, 'wisdom must be shared, it must be given, or else it lies cold upon the rocks. I would give you my wisdom, young one.'"

"And did he?"

"A little, I think. I saw him only once more before I went off to sea. He talked to me again, for a long time."

"He is a strange one," Michael agreed. "The Indians will not speak of him. Whenever I have tried to learn from them who or what he was, they have avoided my questions."

"They probably just don't know," Standish replied dryly. "Nothing mysterious there. He's just an old man who lives alone."

Eileen looked at him. "Win, you're the best nephew a woman ever had . . . but you're not Irish."

"What has that to do with it?" Standish asked, a bit irritated.

"Possibly nothing," she agreed, smiling, "but the Irish are an ancient people, and they do not deny another world."

"Heaven? The Hereafter?" Win said. "Neither do I. I am a churchgoer. I believe in a Heaven and Hell."

"That isn't what I mean," Eileen Mulkerin said, "I mean we Celts are not inclined to be overly skeptical about the Little People, or the mysterious. Ireland was a haunted land, but the ghosts were friendly there, most of them."

"Señora," Standish said, "I cannot understand you. Most of the time you are one of the most practical, sensible, down-to-earth women I have ever known or expect to know, but sometimes—"

She smiled again. "But sometimes I am Irish, is that it?"

"Can you take me to Juan, Jesus?" Sean asked.

"Who knows? I will try."

"Tomorrow, then. Very early."

"What of Wooston?" Michael suggested.

Sean shrugged. "Your problem, Michael. You are a

47

strong man, a sane man, and you are of the Church. If I am here either they or I might become impatient of words, but you can speak, and you are not expected to be violent.

"Let them stay if they insist, but *you* must not go! Stay . . . do not give up possession. That is most important."

"I will go, and—"

"I shall go with you," Eileen Mulkerin said quietly. "It is my ranch, and Juan knows me also. We will both go."

"And I," Mariana said.

"Not you," Sean brushed the suggestion aside with some impatience. "It will be a long ride, a hot, hard ride, and we do not know what will happen nor where it will end."

"You seem to forget, Captain, that Andres will come. He will take me by force, and if you do not want Brother Michael to resist and be killed . . . for Andres would not hesitate, believe me."

"She can ride with me," Eileen said. "She will be company for me, and I do not think she will wilt or fall by the way."

"I grew up on a ranch. I could ride a horse as soon as I could walk."

"This is ridiculous!" Standish protested. "Señora, what are you thinking of? Riding off into the hills after some nameless old Indian who knew your husband!

"He probably knows nothing! In any event, your husband brought home very little gold. Don't you think he would have brought more if there was more? And after all, the old man may be dead."

"Can you suggest an alternative?" the Señora asked quietly. "Win, I know how you feel, but I know of nothing else we can do. Twice before the gold saved us, and maybe it will on this occasion. If we do not do this, what do we do? Give up the ranch? Or turn these hills into a bloody battleground? I will die here, Win Standish, rather than give up a single acre!"

"Oh, all right! Go if you must!" He hesitated. "Will you be all right, Michael? I'd like to ride in and talk to Pio. Maybe there is something he can do . . . or suggest. He is a wise man."

"There's no use asking how long you will be gone," Michael said, "but whatever the time, I shall be here. Have no fear about that."

"Tennison is on the schooner, and he will either be lying at Point Dume, in the cove beside it, or up the coast. You know where. I have told him to preserve the *Lady Luck* at all costs. He will be ghosting off shore if not in close, so a signal will call him."

"I will be all right," Michael said quietly.

"And pray," Sean said. "I think we will need your prayers . . . the more the better."

"You do not pray, Sean?" Michael suggested gently.

Sean grinned. "I'll be praying, don't worry about that! But I am afraid prayers from my lips won't have the appeal yours will."

Sean went to his room and stripped off his shirt and bathed in the basin, pouring cold water from the pitcher. It was good to be back, even at such a time.

The bare, whitewashed walls of his room were home. He could hear faint sounds in the other rooms as the others prepared for bed.

Suddenly his door opened slightly. It was Jesus.

"I think we will be watched," he said, "and followed."

"By Russell?"

Montero shrugged. "By Russell, or by Tomas . . . somebody. After I show you, I shall come back to be with Brother Michael."

"Thank you. I would like that."

Montero closed the door and squatted against the wall. His eyes were very black. "I did not know the Old One had talked with you. If he did so you are chosen."

"What does that mean?"

Montero did not reply for a moment. "They say of him that he was the last of his people, that they were a great people who came here from afar. They say that once there was a city in the desert, a very great city of adobe and stone and it existed for many lifetimes, and then one night there was a great shaking of the earth and after many days it continued to shake and there was no more city, no more people . . . only a handful . . . and Juan, the Old One."

"It's a good story, Montero, but I doubt it. Pedro Fages came up through this country long ago and he spoke of no city. There were others along the coast a hundred years before him, at least. I think it is only a story. How old can Juan be? Is he seventy? Eighty?"

"He is old, Señor, very, very old. Who can say how old? Can you put a time to his years? I cannot. The oldest men of the villages cannot. There was a Chumash who lived on San Miguel. He was very old, and he told me that when he was a child Juan looked as he does now. Who knows, Señor?

"Are you ready to say what can and cannot be? I am not. I am a humble man, Señor, yet I have ridden among the mountains, I have traveled far, far to the south and seen many things. My people call me a wise one . . . a maker of magic . . . but to him I am a child, Señor. I, who am a proud man, confess it.

"You measure time, Señor. I have seen the brass clock on your ship. You are very careful to measure time, and perhaps this is the white man's fault . . . that he tries to measure the immeasurable. That he tries to put chains upon the unchainable. What is time, Señor? Who can say? You count footsteps when you measure land. You count sun and moons and the seasons, but what does it tell you? Do you know, Señor, I think you do wrong to count these things.

"I think they *are*. I think time *is*. I do not think time passes, as you say. I think time is here, that it never began, can never be measured, and will always be.

"I think you walk up and down and across because that is what you believe the world to be, but perhaps there are others who walk up and down and across but also walk through."

"Through? Through what?"

Montero got to his feet. Carefully, he brushed his sombrero. "There is always tomorrow. Now I shall sleep."

"Jesus?"

Montero had lifted the latch on the door. "Sí, Señor?"

"You have talked to the Old One, too?"

"A little, Señor, only a little. Not as he will talk to you. *Buenos noches, Señor. Hasta la vista.*"

The door closed softly behind him and Sean sat down on his bed and pulled off a boot. He dropped it to the floor, then took off the second and held it in his hand, thoughtfully rubbing his foot. Then carefully he placed the second boot on the floor.

Would someone lie awake waiting for the second boot to be dropped?

Were there always two boots?

Was everything always and forever what we expect it to be? Or is that merely a way we have of looking at the world so it is comfortable to live in?

He lay back on the bed, blew out the candle, and closed his eyes.

Chapter 6

Although the hour was early the heat was intense in the narrow canyon. Montero led the way, followed closely by Eileen Mulkerin and behind her, Mariana. They were followed by a couple of packhorses and then Sean.

The horses plodded slowly for the trail was winding and difficult. There was no breeze in the canyon. Several times they saw cattle, wilder than the deer. One magnificent red bull, head up, nostrils flaring, glared at them trying to decide whether to charge, but as they kept on their way, ignoring him, he snorted, threw up his tail, trotted a couple of yards after them, then tossed his head and went off over the hill.

All was still. They heard no sound but the hoofs of their horses and the occasional buzzing of bees. On the narrow, rocky trail they could move but slowly and by midmorning they were no more than ten miles from the ranch. Several times Montero had dropped back to dust over their tracks, doing so each time they passed a branch canyon.

Sean rode with his rifle in his hands. At this point he was expecting no trouble but was aware that it could come at any moment.

His life in the mountains, the desert, and at sea had sharpened his senses until alertness was a way of life. At sea he had learned to sense the slightest change in the movement of the ship through the water, the creak of the rigging, or the slap of a sail.

Yet having grown up herding cattle, riding the range in the rough desert mountains of southern California, one of the greatest cattle raising areas in the world at the time, he knew the wild country in all its moods.

Montero reached a widening of the trail and stopped to let the horses catch a breath. Sean rode to the head of the column.

"How much further?"

Montera shrugged. "Sundown . . . no sooner. It is not far to where the trail branches, a short distance only. We will take the left."

"Isn't that Saddle Rock Peak?" He indicated a clump of rocks atop a low peak some distance off to their right. "I have not ridden this way in a long time."

"It is Saddle Rock . . . and as close as we come. We ride north and a little east."

Sean dismounted and walked his horse back into the shade, seating himself on a rock near the women, who had also gotten down to rest their horses.

"Will he stop to eat?" Mariana asked.

Sean grinned at her. "Hungry? No, I don't think he will . . . yet. He's heading for a place where there's water. Dry as these hills are, there's water if you know where to find it. Montero has handled cattle in these hills long enough to know most of them."

"Not all?"

"Only the old Indians know all of them."

He gestured. "Lobo Canyon lies yonder. I killed my first lion over there. Nine feet long he was and crouched on top of a boulder trying to decide whether I was dangerous or not. I was twelve then, and I guess he decided I was pretty small stuff. His tail was lashing . . . getting set to jump . . . so I shot him."

Once more they started on, following a dim trail westward toward the highest peak in the immediate area, a blunt sandstone shoulder that was part of a long ridge that ended in another bold peak to the west and south.

Suddenly Montero turned north and began to follow a still dimmer trail that seemed to be leading up the sandstone peak itself. Several times Sean saw the tracks of sandals here, and recognized them as those left by the Old One.

He was alive then. The old man was not dead. He felt a curious excitement as well as relief, for all the way along he had been fearing the old man had passed on. How long since he had seen him? It had not been for a long, long time!

The growth thinned out, everywhere there was sandstone. How, he wondered, did the old man live? Where did he get water? What did he eat? Why had he not come down to the ranch where he would have been welcome at any time?

Suddenly they were in a nest of smaller peaks almost atop the ridge. There were some trees here and some brush that was suddenly of a deeper green. They rounded a boulder into a small clearing and there before them, built against the wall of sandstone, was a small hut of woven branches. Part of it woven from still living, growing trees.

On a bench at the door sat Juan, the Old One.

He looked incredibly old, unbelievably frail. He wore a straw hat, a worn serape of many colors, and handwoven sandals.

"How do you do, my friends?" His voice was low but resonant. "You have been long in coming."

"You have been waiting?" Eileen asked.

"Of course. Your husband said that if anything happened to him I was to tell only you . . . or the boy." He looked at Sean. "The boy is a man. It is good."

He waved a hand. "Will you be seated? My home offers little."

They dismounted. Montero led the horses into the

shade, then returned and squatted on his heels and began to smoke a thin cigar.

Sean put a hand on Mariana's elbow. "Old One, this is Mariana de la Cruz. She is from Mexico."

The dark eyes turned to her. "Ah? Of course. I was there once . . . as a boy. A beautiful city, but not what I had expected. We were told it was an island in a lake, but there was no island and not much left of the lake."

They sat around on stones and benches, and the old man went within. When he returned it was with a pitcher of something cold and he filled a small clay cup for each. "It is an old drink, made of chia and honey. It is cooling . . . and it gives strength to the muscles."

"We are in trouble, Juan," the Señora said gently. "Men would take the ranch from us if we do not pay. We thought you might know where my husband found the gold."

"Yes. I know you are in trouble, and I know you came about the gold. I will tell you, and then you must go. You are followed. Eight men follow you. They would kill you, all of you."

"You will come with us?"

"I will come. You could not go alone." He looked at Sean. "And once we have gone, only you may ever come back for gold. Remember . . . only you."

Montero rose. "I will get your horse, Old One."

"*Gracias.*" The old man turned to Eileen. "You do not change, Señora. You are as one of us."

"Us?" she asked gently.

He smiled, amusement stirring the wrinkles at the corners of his eyes. "My people are gone now, Señora, but once we were many. Never so many as you, never so many as most peoples, but enough."

"Your people did not age?"

"All men age, as all men die. The thing is not to die too soon, Señora, and to live wisely. To live a long time is nothing, to live a long time wisely is something."

"You speak well. You are a strange man, Old One."

"I believe unfamiliar is the term, Señora." He paused a moment, watching Montero come up from the rocks behind the hut leading a fine buckskin horse. "Until your husband came I was a lonely man. I needed ears to listen, a voice to reply. The Chumash were a good people, very bright and quick, but their experience was only with our land here. Your husband was a man who had traveled in ideas as well as upon trails and the sea. He listened well, he talked well. He understood much. His was a wide mind, given to acceptance where others might have denied."

"You are an educated man, Old One."

"What is education but a conditioning of the mind to a society and a way of life? There are many kinds of education, and often education closes as many doors as it opens, for to believe implies disbelief. One accepts one kind of belief but closes the mind to all that is, or seems to be contradictory."

Sean was sitting forward, all his attention upon the old man, everything within him suddenly alive. What was it the old man had said to him, those times long ago? He did not remember what was said, only that it had made a difference. He knew now he had never been the same since, that he would never be the same again.

"You said something once about wisdom," he said. "That it must be shared. I would share yours, Old One. If you will talk, I will listen."

"Yes. I will speak. But it is important to listen with all the senses, and to feel. Awareness is a way of learning, too. In these days to come you must be alive and aware to everything. Let the days leave tracks upon your memory."

Suddenly he turned away and walked to the buckskin horse. He gathered the reins, put a hand on the pommel and swung easily to the saddle. He motioned to the others to mount and follow him. Without another word he started along the ridge, then crossed over to the north side.

There seemed no trail beyond that point, but he led on.

He turned in his saddle and spoke to Sean, who now rode behind him while Montero had fallen back to the rear. "Do not forget the way. I am soon to die."

"No."

"Soon."

Sean glanced at his mother. Her cheeks looked gaunt, a little tired. It was the same with Mariana. "Can you make it?"

"Of course," the Señora smiled. "Can you?"

Sean laughed, and Mariana smiled back at him. "Ride on," she said, "you will not leave us behind!"

The wind blew off the sea, and although the sun was hot, the wind kept them cool. At times they rode in the shade of sandstone cliffs, at other times under trees. Twice Sean saw the tracks of grizzlies, different from other bears by the long claws on the forepaws. Once he saw the track of a mountain lion and several times of bighorns.

The old man led them down a narrow, switchback trail. This was an old trail now, into which they had suddenly come. He led them deep into a canyon past huge boulders where water dripped. There were many birds, all chirping at once.

"Water here," the old man said. "It is far."

There were a few minutes of respite in the cool shade where the water fell, it was a lost place, a cool, pleasant place away from the hot sun.

Soon the old man mounted again. "How far?" Sean asked.

The old man merely said, "To the end. To where we go, and it will be like places you have seen, but unlike places you know."

Sean dried his palms on his shirt front and looked down into the deeper canyon. It was nondescript, offering no landmarks. This was a trail that would be easy to lose. The old man was right. One must be aware.

Mariana rode beside the Señora at a place where the trail was wide. "He does not sound like an Indian."

"What is an Indian? There are Aztecs as well as Eskimos. There are Toltecs and Iroquois."

"I like him."

"Yes." They separated as the trail narrowed, drew together again when it widened. "Did you notice that he said nothing when he found we were coming along? He did not even suggest we be left behind."

"He knew better," Eileen said dryly, and then added, "but it is true. Obviously the equality of women has never been an issue among his people . . . or so it would seem."

Topping out on a rise, Sean looked back, mopping the sweat from his forehead. He could see nothing behind him but sandstone heights and shimmering heat waves. Were Machado and his men following?

The Old One had said they were, and in his heart he believed it himself. Perhaps one did not always have to see or hear to know. Perhaps one just *knew*. Was that how the old Indian did it? Even Montero, at times. Was there something on the wind? Did the motion and men and their thoughts create patterns in the air that traveled on until felt by someone attuned to them?

He shrugged. His hand went back to his belt where his pistol was. It was a new-style repeating pistol made in Paterson, New Jersey, and designed by a man named Colt. It was a good pistol, the best of them so far, and called a "long nine" by the man who sold it to him, a man who was broke in Panama.

At the same time Sean had bought his rifle, an eight-shot Colt revolving rifle, and a good one. He had himself tinkered with it a little, setting the sights a bit finer and improving the mechanism.

It was good to be back in the saddle again, and the mustang he rode was a sure-footed mountain horse brought up from Mexico. Several times he glanced back, and once, far away on the sandstone ridge, he thought he caught a flash of sunlight on something metallic. It could have been his imagination.

The sun was sliding rapidly downhill when the old man finally drew up at a spring in the Potrero. "Water your horses and fill your canteens. We'll make a dry camp."

"We're going further?" Sean was worried about his mother and Mariana.

"Only a mile or two. Tomas might know of this spring, although I doubt it."

They let the horses drink deep, then rode away in the gathering darkness. Their camp was a hidden place in a niche of the hills.

There was soft sand there; Sean kicked away a couple of stones and spread blankets for his mother and Mariana. "Better get some sleep. We'll be moving on at daylight."

He watched as Montero led the horses to a patch of grass and picketed them there, then sat down on a rock and looked at the stars. Tonight the old man was not talkative, and after a few minutes Sean saw Montero returning.

"I will watch," Montero said. "Sleep while you can."

"Call me at midnight," he told Montero, and going to a point near the women, who were already asleep, he rolled in his blanket with his weapons beside him and stretched out.

He tried to sleep, but for awhile sleep would not come. The stars seemed very near, very bright. The night was soft as a maiden's touch, and there was only a suggestion of a breeze.

He heard a pebble fall among stones, the brief stirring of some small animal and when next he awakened Montero was beside him.

He sat up quickly. "What is it?"

"I am sleepy, amigo. It is time for you to watch."

Sean shook out his boots carefully. He had no desire to put a foot into a boot with a tarantula or scorpion in it. Then he stood up, shook out his blankets, rolled them behind his saddle, and taking up his rifle, listened to Montero.

"It is quiet. I do not believe they are close, but be careful."

"What about Indians?"

Jesus shrugged. "No California Indian would come near us when the Old One is along . . . and they know he is here. I can't answer for raiders from across the Colorado, the Mohaves or Paiutes from the north."

An hour passed, and then another. Sean circled the camp several times, checked the horses, and then returned to the campsite. He had seated himself on a rock when his mother joined him.

"I am awake, Sean, if you wish to sleep."

"It is all right. I slept well."

"We must save the ranch, Sean. Somehow it must be saved."

"We will."

"I know." She sat down near him. "Mariana is a lovely girl."

"Yes."

"You are in love with her?"

He chuckled. "There's been no time for romance. Too much to worry about. She is lovely, though, and if the ranch were free and clear—"

"There is time. I think she will be with us for a long while, Sean."

He said nothing, listening into the night. There seemed a sudden, heavier stillness. He waited, expecting he knew not what.

He glanced at his mother. She was sitting a little straighter, looking down the valley toward the spring.

"Somebody is coming," she said.

Chapter 7

Suddenly Juan was near them. "Come, we will go now."

Montero had brought their horses, and once mounted Juan turned sharply away from the way they had come and led them into what appeared to be a solid wall of chaparral, higher than their heads.

There was, in fact, a trail. The brush closed in on either side, the leaves brushing their knees and stirrups, sometimes their shoulders. Juan wasted no time. The old man led the way into the tangle like a young vaquero after an old mossyhorn steer.

In single file, they followed. Weaving and winding

through the dark passage, able to see no further than their mounts' ears, maintaining absolute silence aside from the small sounds of their passing.

At a small clearing in the brush the Old One pulled up long enough for Montero to drop back to the rear, then they moved on. Suddenly, Sean realized the air was growing lighter . . . the moon was rising.

Emerging from the brush they dipped into a deeply shadowed canyon. Juan held his pace. Above them the mountains loomed, dark and mysterious, and before them the canyon was black, showing nothing.

After an hour of riding they emerged into a wide, moonlit valley, but the old man wasted no time, riding out into the valley and pointing the way diagonally across it.

Here the grass was brown and parched. There was dust, and silence.

For two miles or more they stayed with the valley, then pointing at a rocky tower before them they skirted it and entered a narrow draw.

Steadily they rode and suddenly emerged from the draw into a wide place where there were cottonwoods, an old adobe house, now fallen to ruin, and a pole corral.

"We will stop here," Juan said "for one hour of rest."

"I will ride back and watch the valley," Montero said, and was gone.

Sean helped his mother from the saddle, although she needed none of it. "Help yourself," she said, "I have ridden further than this."

"We have further to go," he said quietly.

"What do you know? Juan will tell us."

"It is further?" Mariana asked.

The old man smiled. "Three days, if all goes well. Possibly four. You will come?"

"Of course," Eileen Mulkerin said. "Did you think we would stop?"

"Can we have coffee, Old One? Or is a fire dangerous?"

"It would be good." He squatted on his heels near a rock. "They will not find where we have come until daybreak, I think. The path through the brush is not much."

"Old One," Sean said carefully, "one of those who rides with Tomas once rode with Vasquez, the outlaw. He knows the trails."

The old man looked up. "There are some trails a man can ride that can be ridden by no other. Let them follow if they dare."

Sean made a small fire and got a coffeepot from a packhorse. In a few minutes he had water boiling. Eileen took over then and made the coffee, and he walked out away from their group to listen.

It was very quiet.

The Old One knew what he was doing, but Sean liked none of it. Tomas Alexander's cantina was a stopping place for all who rode through, and many were outlaws from the gangs of Vasquez or one of the several Joaquins. Tomas knew the back trails himself and had men with him who knew, too.

If caught out in these lonely hills where Californios rarely came, they would hesitate at nothing. Juan was unarmed, Montero had an old Hawken rifle, while his mother had a Colt revolving rifle like his own. Mariana was not armed.

In a fight it would be Montero, his mother, and himself.

Machado would have Russell, Tomas, and others.

To avoid a fight was the logical conclusion, and that was what Juan seemed inclined to do.

Eileen Mulkerin stood by the campfire and studied her son. Somehow it seemed odd to think of him in that light, for in many ways this broad-shouldered young man was a stranger to her.

Michael, for all his youthful wildness, had always been closer to home. It was Sean, the steady one, who had gone out upon the deep water with Jaime and with others, and who had come back to her from time to time, stronger, more assured, and with a ringing voice of command that startled her at times.

Yet he had a vein of something else, too. Some might have said it was the sea except for the fact that it was the same quality, a strain of mysticism, that had turned Michael toward the Church.

Jaime had had it too, and she did herself. It was Celtic, deep within them all, yet deeper and stronger in Sean perhaps than in any of them. Montero had mentioned it once when he was speaking of Sean as a boy. Old Juan had seen it, too.

What were the things that made up a man? Was it only hard fists and a salty way? Was it a strain of gentleness, a love of the land? Or was it so much else?

In these last hours of the night she looked again at the sky, growing faintly pale now along the eastern rim of the mountains. A few stars still hung in the sky like distant harbor lights, and the blackness in the deepest canyon remained.

She crossed to where the old man sat, and he looked up as she approached. He started to rise, but she gestured for him to stay. "I will sit," she said.

Juan looked older, even quieter if that was possible. Yet something was different about him. "What is it, Juan?"

"There will be blood," he said quietly, "blood and death. You should not have come."

"Since when was a woman afraid of blood?" she asked. "The problem is not only Sean's. It is mine also. If there is to be blood, I will share in the letting or the losing of it."

He shook his head. "There is no end. Man was born in travail, and in travail he lives."

"This place to which we go? Will there be safety there? Shelter?"

"There is no safety upon this earth, and no shelter but for a time. There was once a time when my people had shelter, and in a night, it was gone, and in the days and weeks that followed there was not even a stone laying upon a stone that was not shaken down.

"We lived in a world of our making. We had learned things beyond the ways of men, and we believed ourselves secure. We were not secure.

"We had wisdom of a sort. We knew not the things you and your people know, but we knew much else that you do not know, perhaps cannot know, yet it was of no use. The earth trembled and cracked and dust arose, and there was fire, and my people fled, fled they knew not where. Some went to the sea and died there in great waves that followed the fifth week of trembling, and some went to the desert and died of thirst, and many lay dead in the ruins of all we had built.

"A few of us went to the mountains. Some of us lived. Many died because they knew not how to live without all they had had about them. I was young. I was a priest among them, but I was also one who loved the wild lands and often went out to search for herbs for medicines, so I lived."

"I have never heard of this." She looked at him, wondering. "Did you ever tell Jaime of this?"

"A little. He found a wall once, in the desert, and beside the wall some broken bits of a pot. It was thin, fragile, beautiful. He wondered how a Chinese pot could come here and was surprised when I told him the piece was not of China, but a fragment of our own. We talked a little then."

"And Sean? Does he know of this?"

The old man was silent for several minutes, and then he said, "He knows much by himself. He perceives. He feels. He knows where something has taken place, where things have been. It is something deep within him."

"You taught him something when he was much younger?"

"Taught? Perhaps. All teaching is not instruction, sometimes it is only opening a door or lifting a veil. Lift the veil and one does not need to teach for the mind sees, realizes, understands."

"You spoke of blood? Will my son survive the blood-letting?"

"I do not know, Señora. Once I was young, and I knew many things, but now the light burns low and what I perceive is but dimly as through a curtain."

"And your city? The place from which you came? Your people? Who were they?"

"Another people . . . it does not matter now. I am the last of us, I believe, and I am old, so very old."

"But where did you come from?"

"Elsewhere, but long, long ago. It does not matter, Señora, and I speak of this to no one."

"Not even to Sean?"

"Not yet . . . soon, perhaps. But only a little. The past is gone. My people who were proud and strong and fierce went down as does the grass before the fire. We were once here, and there was dust and smoke, and there was no more of us."

"You should tell someone what you know. There should be a history, so that men can learn from it."

He smiled. "Men do not learn from history. Each generation believes itself brighter than the last, each believes it can survive the mistakes of the older ones. Each discovers each old thing and they throw up their hands and say 'See! Look what I have found! Look upon what I know!' And each believes it is something new.

"We had them in plenty, the new discoverers, exclaiming with excitement over what we had long ago tested and found false. We had the greedy ones, too, and those who wished for power or to show power. They are gone now, with all the rest.

"Once a priest talked to me. He spoke long of the sins of this world and wished me to declare for his god that all my sins be remitted. I listened to him patiently and smiled inside for I had no sins to be forgotten and none to be forgiven. He told me of Sodom and Gomorrah, and I listened and felt a sadness upon me, for what had happened to us had happened there also."

The last of the stars had disappeared. The old man got to his feet. "We must go now. I do not know how, but they have found a way and they are close . . . much too close."

She went to Sean. "Juan says they are coming, and he says there will be blood."

"I have been expecting it."

Once more they merged with the beginning day, lending their movements to the vanishing shadows and the growing light, riding along the faces of slopes like cloud shadows under the sun, and leaving no mark upon the land they left behind.

Sean dried his hands on his shirt again and turned his head to look at the hills behind them. Nothing . . . yet.

He knew it was coming and rode warily, sitting light

in the saddle, ready to kick free of the stirrups and drop to the ground if need be. He wanted no wasted shots, no galloping horse beneath him. He could shoot from the saddle, and had done it many times, but this time he must be sure, and with each shot a man must fall. His mother was here, and Mariana.

The old man set a killing pace. On through the sun-blasted hills he rode, winding up on the long slopes, along the ridges and into strange canyons. He waded their horses through streams, pushed through thickets, turned and doubled and changed his direction again and again.

Once, far back, Sean thought he saw dust, but Juan shook his head. "I do not know what dust that is, but it is not theirs. They are closer. They simply do not see us."

Sean saw, once in awhile, a deer track. He saw no others. Yet within the last mile or so the terrain had suddenly changed, for he was weaving a way through canyons of up-tilted strata, great layers of rock broken and thrust sharply upward, the edges only beginning to be worn by wind and blown sand. It was a nightmare of broken ledges, twisted rocks, deep gorges, and desolation.

He spoke of it to Montero.

"It is a great crack," the Mexican said, "a crack in the earth that cuts through the mountains for many miles, from Mexico to the sea far north of Monterey. At places the trail follows the bottom, and I have ridden it."

"An earthquake fault," Sean commented. "I've heard of such places."

It was dark when again they stopped, and Juan drew up and got stiffly down. "Do not unsaddle. We will make coffee, eat, and ride on."

"Tonight?" Mariana was incredulous.

"We must."

When they had eaten and had drunk their coffee, Juan got more slowly to his feet. Sean looked at him, suddenly worried. "Perhaps we should rest, Old One. You are tired."

Juan shrugged. "These days I am often tired. It is no matter."

"But a little rest—?"

"There is no time. They come quickly."

As Sean moved to put out the fire, the old man stopped him. "No, add wood, and leave it burning. They will believe that we are here. They will get down, creep up, and find nothing. Nothing at all."

"And so?"

"We shall have gained a few miles, perhaps a whole night. It is a difference, amigo."

Wearily they mounted, and wearily Juan led them into the night, into the darkness.

Chapter 8

It was daylight before they again stopped. The place was a canyon with towering walls that went steeply up, then sloped back. There were junipers there, and piñon pine.

"We will rest," Juan said.

He squatted against a boulder. "We cannot go on. They are too close."

"Close? How do you know? We have seen nothing!"

"I know."

"We must have the gold, Juan. We will lose the ranch."

"Is it so important? It is land, but there is much

land. If you lose that, go elsewhere and take more. I can show you more land, finer land."

"It is our home. The mountains are there, and the sea. Our schooner is there. The grave of my father is there."

"Ah, yes. I had forgotten that." He paused, then said. "They are too close. They will find us and they will take it all."

"They will take nothing." Eileen Mulkerin said flatly. "They will take nothing, Juan. They will get nothing but trouble. I will not lose the place, Juan. I will not lose it, do you hear?"

"Those men who follow? They are bad men?"

"The worst."

Eileen Mulkerin spoke. "There is the one called Wooston, and there is King-Pin Russell, Tomas Alexander, and Jorge Fernandez."

"Fernandez? A thin, hard man?"

"Sí . . . and there is Andres Machado."

Juan stirred the sand with a stick. "This Fernandez . . . I know of him. He killed a girl, I think. An Indian girl?"

"He is the one."

"She was known to me. Sometimes she brought me *frijoles* . . . she was a good girl."

He sat silent, then shook his head. "No. I cannot. You are my friends. I know that. But this is not what you think. It is no great treasure, but only a little gold, not easily had. For you there might be enough . . . but I cannot risk it."

Sean squatted, too. "Old One? Take them. I will stay here. I will be sure that no one follows you."

"They will kill you."

"Not until I have killed them. You take the Señora and Mariana . . . go. I will stay."

70

"If you stay," Montero said, "I will stay with you."

The Old One looked from one to the other, slowly shaking his head. "You are brave men, good men." He paused again, then sighed and shook his head. "Rest a little then. Let the horses roll, take them to drink in the hole beyond the bushes. We must go soon."

He moved away from them and, curling up in a shadow, went to sleep.

Eileen Mulkerin looked at her son. "We should not do this, Sean. I think the place he is taking us to is very special. Possibly a sacred place."

"You are probably right, and I am worried for him, but what I have said, I will do. You ride on with him. I shall stay."

"We all go . . . or none."

"Señora, I—"

"No. I have spoken. That is how it will be. I love the ranch, but the ranch is not worth my son's blood. I say no . . . all go, or none."

He knew better than to argue. "What about the gold?" he asked. "Was it melted down or was it ore?"

"I never saw it."

Montero led the horses away and Sean leaned back against a rock. He was tired, very tired. The long voyage, the worry, and now this. His eyes closed. He opened and shut his fingers, closing them into fists.

Somehow, somehow he must save them all. Juan, his mother, Mariana.

Montero? He was a good man, and together they would do what must be done. They were men, and they would stand together. What happened remained in the hands of God . . . or destiny.

Suddenly he felt a hand on his shoulder and opened his eyes. The sun was high in the sky, and the hand was Juan's. "You sleep well, my son. It is time to ride."

"Could you not tell us where to go? You could hide nearby and rest."

"The road I travel is one of memories. It is good for me to go."

"My husband had much respect for you," Eileen Mulkerin said.

"He was a good man, Señora. He had respect for the old ways and when the old gods spoke to him, he listened."

"The old gods?"

"They are here, in all the quiet places. If you are silent in the wilderness they will, in time, come close to you. If you respect their world they will come to love you.

"Those who follow us, they know not what they do." Juan glanced at her. "You are known to the Old Ones. They know you belonged to him, and you are a quiet woman—"

She laughed. "You do not know me, Juan, or you would not say that. I am a hard, bold, demanding woman."

He shrugged. "You know to be silent in the wilderness. It is that which matters, to learn to live with silence."

He walked to his horse. "It is time now. We must go."

Andres Machado was in the lead when they reached the place of the fire. He rode quickly around, then back. Russell followed him. "This was the smoke we saw. What do you suppose it was for?"

Machado shrugged. "Coffee." He swung down from the saddle, a lithe man, easy in his movements. "We will have some ourselves." He turned. "Silva! We will have food now."

"It was a signal," Silva muttered.

They all looked at him. "A signal? To whom?"

He shrugged. "They cooked. There is spattered grease and a few coffee grounds from an emptied cup. But it was a signal, too."

"Who could he signal to?" Alexander asked, impatiently. "There is nobody out here, Silva. Not even Indians live in this wilderness."

"It was a signal," Silva insisted.

"What about that old Indian?" Wooston asked. "I only saw him once, but he had some tie-up with Mulkerin."

"I do not know him," Tomas said, looking away.

"I saw him once," Fernandez spoke reluctantly. "He was strange . . . he was an old one."

"Strange? How?"

"Well, just strange. Kept to himself. Never came into town. The other Indians fought shy of him, never seemed easy around him, almost like they were scared."

"What's to be scared of?" Russell asked, contemptuously. "I seen him once. Just an old man . . . looked to be a hundred years old. Good puff of smoke could blow him away."

Tomas lifted his black eyes to Russell. He did not like him very much. "But none has," he said. "In a hundred years a man sees much smoke."

Silva was slicing bacon into a pan. "They say he can call up the spirits . . . that he can will things to happen."

Russell laughed. "Nonsense! That's pure nonsense!"

They sat together, dozing and talking. Wooston, Russell, Alexander, Fernandez, and Andres Machado. Their party had grown in size, and among the additions were a dozen Californios, of whom Silva was one.

Silva was a short, square-shouldered man, three-quarters Indian, one-quarter Spanish. He was a good cook, an excellent vaquero, and a tracker. Few of the Californios had any use for wild country, but Silva was an exception, as Pedro Fages and Father Garces had been.

"What you figure on doin' when we catch 'em?" Russell asked, glancing at Machado.

"It is a wild country," Wooston said, "it's easy to get lost out here. Be surprisin' if they ever found their way back."

Russell took a cigar from his vest pocket. "Be a real surprise to me," he said. "Any number of accidents can happen."

Machado looked at them with distaste. "Your business is your business," he said shortly. "I want that girl and a whip. That is all."

"And Sean Mulkerin? Who stole your woman?"

"I do not know that he stole her. She fled . . . it was some silly girl's whim . . . and it was his boat. However," he added, "I shall fight him and kill him."

"Better just kill him," Russell advised.

"Him?" Machado sneered. "I never liked him, anyway. No, I shall fight him and kill him. It would give me great satisfaction."

Tomas glanced at Machado. "Be careful, Señor. He is very strong, a good fighter. If I were you, I would shoot him . . . from far off. When he falls I would shoot into him five more times, just to be sure."

Machado snorted, and reached into the pan for a strip of bacon.

Tomas went on. "In my cantina one night . . . it was only last year . . . five men from another ship decided to rob him. Mulkerin was coming up from the shore with the money from the sale of a cargo. These were bad men. And they started a fight with him."

"I remember somethin' about that," Wooston said. "Killed a couple of them, didn't he?"

"I cannot afford to have killings at my cantina," Tomas replied gravely, "so bodies are never found there. However, two bodies were found on the road near the cienaga . . . and there were two other men who became somehow disabled."

"And the other?"

"He ran, Señor. He had less courage but greater wisdom. Capitan Mulkerin had a few scratches, I think, and skinned knuckles."

"Knives," Machado said. "They should have used knives."

"Two of them tried, Señor Machado. Two of them tried very hard with knives. One died with his own knife in his ribs, the other had a broken arm and collarbone."

It was a somber day. Low gray clouds lay upon the mountains, shrouding the peaks and the higher ridges. The canyons were silent, awesome, haunted.

When they started out again, Fernandez led off. But he had gone only a short distance when he drew up sharply.

"What is it?" Machado demanded impatiently.

Fernandez pointed.

Two crossed sticks lay in the trail.

"Well? What of it?" Wooston demanded, as they bunched around.

"I do not like it," Fernandez said. "It is a sign."

"Bah!" Machado said contemptuously. "We waste time!" He rode over the sticks and on down the trail, and the others followed.

From high in the rocks above them there came a weird, lonely howl, a howl that sent chills up their spines. Once more they drew up, guns in hand. The howl rose, died away, then lifted again.

Their eyes searched the rocks above them, but they saw nothing.

"Coyote," Russell said.

"That?" Tomas stared at him. "That was no coyote. It was a soul of the dead, a lost soul."

Wooston laughed. "Well, I ain't afraid of no ghosts. Let's go."

One of Machado's men was in the lead. Suddenly, they saw his horse rear wildly, and the man drew his pistol and fired.

Rushing up, they saw nothing.

"What's the matter?" Wooston demanded. "You gone crazy?"

"There was a snake, a big rattler, right in the trail."

"Well? Where is he now?"

There was no snake, no winding trail in the dust, nothing.

Tomas glanced uneasily at Silva, who shrugged.

"There was a snake!" The man repeated stubbornly. "I saw it. So did my horse."

"So? Ain't you never seen a snake before? Let's go!" Russell was impatient.

With a glance of contempt, Machado rode past into the lead. The trail wound down a long, shallow draw, dusty and dry, with scattered rocks and cacti. Suddenly Machado stopped, waiting for Silva. "The trail is gone," he said. "Find it."

Silva rode on past and began casting back and forth for the lost trail.

"Be dark soon," Russell muttered.

The way grew increasingly rugged. Now the junipers were giving way to scattered pines, and along the streams the sycamores were larger, older, and in greater number.

"Looks like open place up ahead," Wooston said. "We'd better camp."

Silva had picked up the trail, then lost it again. He led them now down into a flat place near a stream where there were several large sycamores. He glanced around uneasily.

"What place is this?" Machado asked.

Silva shrugged. "The stream, I think, is the Sespe. This place, I have heard of it before. It is a bad place."

"Looks good to me," Wooston swung down.

"There has been death here," Silva said. "I was told of this place."

"Forget it," Wooston said, "this here's as good a camp as we're likely to find." He turned toward Silva. "They far ahead of us?"

Silva hesitated, thinking. Then he shrugged. "Maybe an hour, two hours. No more."

"What's wrong?" Wooston's eyes searched Silva's.

"I do not like this place," Silva said, "and something is wrong."

"Wrong? How?"

"The Old One leads them. He guides them."

"So?"

"Something is wrong, Señor. He no longer tries to get away."

"What's that mean?" Wooston was frowning and King-Pin Russell had stopped loosening his saddle to listen.

"If he no longer tries to get away it is because he wishes us to catch up, and if he wishes us to catch up, there may be a trap, no?"

"Trap, Hell! Any trap will be for them, not us."

Russell turned to Silva. "A trap? Now where would they be likely to try that?"

Silva hesitated, looking from one to the other. "This place," he said, "I think this is the place. This is the trap."

Chapter 9

Shortly before noon the Old One led them to a creek. "We will rest for a few minutes and water our horses."

Sean glanced up at the mountainous ridge before them.

Judging from the growth they were probably three thousand feet or so above sea level, and at a guess the ridge before them, running roughly east and west, was three to four thousand feet higher.

He crossed to his mother. She was kneeling by the stream, washing the dust from her face with a damp cloth.

"I think we are close," he said.

"You are right." He extended a hand and she took it and rose. "I wonder why he stopped?"

"To rest, he said."

She glanced around. "He is gone. So is Montero."

Sean turned quickly. The horses were there, but the two old men were gone.

Mariana came to them. "Is this the place?"

"No," Sean said, "but I am trying to decide where we are." He nodded ahead. "That could be Pine Mountain . . . and if it is, this might be the Piedra Blanca."

"You do not know?" Mariana asked.

He shrugged. "There are no maps of this country. Men give names to places, but who knows which creek is the one named? Who knows which mountain? Sometimes a man would name creeks and mountains and then another would come who did not know about the first one and he would name them all over again."

They waited beside the creek, resting and talking in a desultory fashion.

Sean was nervous and worried. From time to time he walked back toward the way they had come, but the trail was visible for only a hundred yards or so. He checked his guns again and again.

Suddenly they reappeared, Montero coming down off the rocks into the little hollow. Immediately he went to his horse and tightened the cinch. "We go now," he said.

Juan appeared a moment later and they rode off up a steep, winding trail that led into a notch in the mountain wall that had once been a stream bed.

The area was thick with forest. Several times they saw Indian writing, faded and old, upon rocks. Twice deer ran away before them. The gorge narrowed until they rode single file, each horse scrambling up the slippery, water-worn rocks in turn.

They topped out suddenly on a long plateau or mesa, scattered with trees, but mostly covered with yellowing grass. They saw deep tracks, and nothing else. Juan led out, riding straight across the mesa toward the northwest. He dipped down through the trees and drew up on a sandy shore beside a running creek. Opposite there was a high, rocky wall, around them a ring of such walls.

"We will stop here," he said, and got down.

It was a quiet place, haunted yet beautiful. The cottonwood leaves rustled gently and spread wide over the hard-packed earth and sand, offering shade and shelter. There was a spring among some rocks that flowed down toward the creek. On the far side were the fallen walls of a stone cabin of some kind, only a few stones remaining in place.

"We will camp," Juan said, "and you and you," he indicated Sean and Mariana, "will stay."

"And I?" Eileen Mulkerin asked.

"You will come."

"I don't like the idea," Sean protested, "we should stay together."

"She will be safe."

"How long will you be gone?"

"Until daybreak, perhaps a little longer. I will tell only her . . . for now. You ride, you shoot, you sail about on the big water . . . perhaps tomorrow you die. I will tell her."

His mother took her rifle and turned to them, smiling. "I'll be all right."

Juan started off, Eileen Mulkerin following.

"I'll be all right," Mariana said, "if you wish to follow them."

"Follow *him?* He would know, somehow. He always knows. If he says stay, we stay."

"I will make coffee."

Montero stripped the saddles from the horses as Sean began to gather wood.

Several times Sean paused to listen and to look around. There were no deer tracks here, no tracks at all. The realization worried Sean, although he did not know why. Twice, in gathering wood, he saw arrowheads. They were longer, slimmer than any he had seen before, and beautifully worked. Stooping to pick up a stick he saw an egg-shell thin bit of pottery. It crumbled to dust in his fingers.

"What kind of a place is this?" he asked Montero.

The Californio shrugged. "It is a place in which to be still," he said briefly. Then after a moment, because after all he had known Sean since he was a child, he said, "It is a place of the Old Ones."

Sean glanced at him, then strolled back to where Mariana had started the coffee. "Don't wander around," he said to her. "Stay close to the fire and the horses."

"You think there will be trouble?"

"Not yet, but this place is eerie. Don't you feel it?"

"It is quiet."

"I wonder where they went."

"After the gold, I suppose. Better stay back under the trees. If anyone should come up they'd not be likely to see you."

"What about you?"

"I thought I'd look around the ruins, over there."

"I'll come with you then."

Montero spoke. "Señor, I would not go over there. It is not a good place. Under the trees is best, or near the fire."

"All right." Sean glanced again at the ruins, puzzled. Not a good place? Superstition, probably. There was a lot of it among the Indians and some of the Californios.

This place was far from any he remembered. There had always been talk, of course. Here and there some hunter of wild horses had penetrated this wild country and returned with stories, and occasionally trappers had added their bit. But actually very little was known.

Sean paced uneasily, aware that somewhere, not too far off, Machado and the others would be searching for them. Wild as the country was, and scarce as trails were, they might still be found, and he had no desire for a pitched battle in such a place as this with Mariana and his mother along.

Jesus Montero was an old but careful man, and a good shot. He was not the kind to pull out when the going was rough. Nor was his mother, that stubborn woman.

"Let's cook up now," he suggested, "then we'll eat and put out the fire. No point helping them find us."

Montero agreed, but took over the cooking himself. Sean wandered about, studying the rim and places

81

where he could be without offering a target. He avoided the ruins because he had no wish to anger Montero. He liked the old man and respected his wishes.

Yet he grew more uneasy. Twice he climbed out of the basin, and from the rim above, studied the country around. There were too many concealed approaches, too many places men could hide.

When Sean returned to the fire, there were tortillas, bacon, and coffee. As they ate, he talked to Mariana. She was, he decided, not only beautiful but also uncommonly sensible.

"You said he was an Indian? The Old One?"

"Who knows? We call him Juan, and my father called him that, but whether it is his name or not, we'll never know. Nor will we know whether he is Mexican, Indian, or Anglo. I think he's Indian, but as I've said, of some tribe we do not know. He's supposed to be from a vanished people."

"We have those in Mexico. Vanished people, I mean."

"Indian wars . . . they were always fighting, just like our ancestors were in Europe, only the tribes were not large and if too many men were lost the tribe died out."

"Will she be all right with him?"

"The Señora? She will. She can take care of herself. But the old man, he would die for her."

"You call her the Señora when she is your mother. Why?"

"Stay around awhile and you'll see. She is the Señora, believe me, she is. Rarely raises her voice but everybody know who's boss. She was that way with everybody but Pa. Everybody called her the Señora. They still do."

He checked his gun again. "I wish Mike was here."

"Mike? You mean your brother Michael?"

"Sure. He's hell-on-wheels with a gun or a rope and can ride anything that wears hair. I know he's gone peaceful, the Church and all that, but sometimes I wonder how peaceful."

Somewhere up in the rocks, an owl hooted.

"You'd better get some sleep. If they've found anything we may ride out of here early in the morning."

"I am not tired."

"After that ride? You get some rest."

"My father ran cattle in the mountains of Guerrero. I have ridden much further."

"Can you use a gun?"

"You ask me that? Of course." Then, reflectively, "Andres would not have liked me, anyway. He did not know what he was asking for. When he saw me all dressed, he did not know that I could ride and shoot like any vaquero. He would not have found me so easy to handle."

"You must sleep. It will be after daylight, they said, before they are back."

In the darkness there was no sound but the leaves and the water. No birds, no frogs.

Mariana walked deeper into the shadows and lay down on her blanket, using her saddle for a pillow. Sean followed and covered her with a poncho.

"You're nice."

He looked at her a moment. "Thanks."

She closed her eyes and listened to the slight jingle of his spurs as he walked back to the fire. He thrust sticks into the coals, just enough to keep it alive and then walked away. She listened to the sound of his crunching steps on the sand. It was a friendly, pleasant sound. She snuggled down under the poncho and slept.

He stood in the shadows some fifty feet away and listened. Mentally he sorted out the sounds of the night. Each place had its own sounds, only here there were fewer. What was there about this place?

There were people who believed that the sorrow or happiness or fear of people who had lived in a place left their mark upon it. He had known houses that were always damp and cold, houses that never seemed to be warm, and there were others that one felt to be home the moment one went through the door.

There had been frightful happenings in some places, and people said a mark was left upon them. Had that happened here? Or was it something else?

He had grown up to stories of the strange and mysterious, both from his mother and from the Indians. The Celts had a strain of darkness and mystery in their blood . . . was it that?

Unexplainable things happened. He had known a few of them at sea, and then there was that time when he had gone ashore in Pegu . . . over Burma way. He had talked to an old man in a ruined temple—

Something was stirring out there in the darkness. Like a shadow, holding close to the rocks, he moved back.

Montero was there. "I heard it, too," he said, "but we must wait. It might be one of the others."

Only a few miles away, Juan had stopped. He had led the way to a high meadow rimmed with low, boulder-strewn hills. They were nearly at the top of the range, she decided.

"The horses will be safe here."

"We are to walk?"

"Only a little way." He paused. "Señora? There is not much gold, I think. Maybe there is not enough. I do

84

not know what gold means to you, or how much it would take."

"Can we be back after daybreak?"

"You are afraid for them?"

"Sean is strong. He is a very good fighter, I have heard, but there are many of them."

"He will not be alone."

"You mean Mariana? And Jesus?"

"There are others."

"Others?"

"You are very young, Señora. I am very old, very, very old. Who knows what others there are, out here in the silences? We who are very old are closer to Them than you."

"I do not understand."

"Some say this place is haunted, and the place where I left them, but the ways of evil are always haunted, and evil breeds its own destruction. I think that is so, Señora."

She did not reply, and after a moment, he spoke again.

"The mind is fed by the imagination and the imagination feeds upon the intangible. Men have seen things and heard things and such things remain in their minds. These things breed fear, worry, a desire to be away, far away."

"You do not talk like an Indian, Juan."

"What is an Indian? How does an Indian talk? An Indian is someone to whom the word seems to apply. It says no more than that, Señora. An Indian can be anything or anybody. You whites have just come, but what you call Indians came not long before you. Before them there were other peoples, and who knows who was the first?

"The land belongs to those who live upon it, Señora,

and people come and go. We will not be the last, you and I, and these about us."

"You spoke of evil as though it had a power in it-self?"

"Does it not? Once there was a city out there, and the city became evil, and perhaps it was the evil it created that destroyed it. And perhaps it was just a changing of the earth. I am all that is left."

"Someday," she said quietly, "you must tell me all you remember. We know of the Aztecs and the Incas, but not of this place you mention."

"The Aztecs and Incas were not old people. They were newcomers. The Aztecs marched down from the north and settled in the reed beds around the lake. After awhile they grew strong and defeated many other peoples. The Incas were upstarts also, building on what had been done before." He chuckled. "But then, we all do that. But I am only an old Indian and have nothing to say that needs to be remembered. You must rest, Señora. Tomorrow we will go the last few steps."

"Can't we go now?"

"Does gold smell? Does it taste? It must be seen, Señora, and for that there must be light. Sleep, now."

Chapter 10

A hand touched Mariana's shoulder and she awakened instantly. Sean was squatting beside her. "Better wake up. I think they are coming now."

"The Señora?"

"The others." He glanced at the glowing coals. "Stay out of sight. I do not want them to know who is here or how many."

She got up quickly and took up her saddle and blanket, carrying them into the shadows. Sean took the saddle from her, and the blanket. Quickly, he saddled her horse. "Don't get too far from your horse, and if the worst comes, ride out of here, and fast. Go to Los Angeles and see Pio Pico. Tell him the story."

He walked back to the edge of the darkness.

The moon was up and the small clearing was bathed in light. From down the canyon there was a click of a hoof on stone, a stir of movement, and they came forward riding in a tight bunch. There were nine or ten of them. Too many.

Sean's position was excellent. He had fairly good cover, and his body merged with the trees and rocks behind him. On his left and some twenty yards off was Mariana, and with her, the horses. Montero had disappeared, but he was not worried about Montero. He would be where it was best for him to be.

They came on, walking their horses. The shadows from the moon, the trees and weird rock formations made a mystery of the darkness.

"I can smell smoke," Russell said.

"There's a fire," someone else said. "It is almost out."

"You are near enough," Sean spoke in a conversational tone, making no effort at a threat. "Just stand where you are."

"Who is it?"

"Sean Mulkerin speaking, and you have come a long way to ride back with nothing."

"We'll see about that," Wooston's voice was flat and harsh.

"Where is Mariana de la Cruz?" Machado asked.

"She has made a decision. She does not wish to marry you."

Machado laughed with contempt. "Women do not

make decisions. Her uncle consented, and it is enough. We have laws, gringo."

"Good laws they are," Sean replied quietly. "I obey them. Do you? And do not think to offend me by calling me gringo. I do not mind the name. And I am as good a Mexican as you are, Machado, whose mother was a Greek."

"You talk a great deal, gringo."

"I know a great deal . . . about all of you."

"Where is she, gringo?" Machado shook out a coiled whip. "I've brought this for her."

They started to spread out a little. Sean laughed. "They do not want to be close to you, Machado. They think you will be first to die."

"I am not afraid."

"Of course not, Machado. Neither are you a fool. Do you wish to be killed for a girl who ran away from you? It would be foolish, amigo. My advice is to withdraw."

"Señora?" Wooston called.

"Nobody talks but me," Sean said. "It was agreed."

"Señora? Give us the gold and you may all go free. I promise it."

"Do you think she would take the word of a thief?" Sean asked contemptuously.

"You call me a thief?"

"You are here. If you are not a thief, why are you here?"

"I think he is alone," Russell said suddenly. "Let's take him."

In the deep shadows, Mariana clicked one stone against another. It sounded somewhat like a rifle bolt.

From high in the rocks there came two more such sounds. One was definitely a rifle being cocked.

"See?" Sean said. "I am not alone, but if you wish to

die for nothing, come. I can kill two, at this range, before you even move."

Machado liked none of this. They were out in the open clearing with the moonlight on them. The sounds had come from widely spaced positions.

"Come!" Machado turned his horse. "It will soon be daylight and they cannot escape."

Slowly, they rode back into the canyon. A hundred and fifty yards away, they drew up. "We can wait here," Machado said.

"Hell," Russell scoffed. "We could have taken 'em! Who can there be? Two women, an old man, and Mulkerin."

Machado looked up at him. "Do not be a fool, Russell. I happen to know that Sean Mulkerin is a fighter. And a dead shot. It is said that the widow is also a good shot. And there is the other man. I do not know about him."

"Montero can shoot," Silva said shortly. "He is a brave man. He moves like a ghost."

Somebody laughed.

Wooston turned sharply. "Who laughed?"

Wooston glared around, from one to the other, but nobody spoke.

It was Silva, finally, who said, "The Old One may be a ghost. Who knows?"

"If we find him, we shall see," Russell said grimly. "I'll find out if a ghost can bleed."

A small rock fell, bouncing from rock to rock in the silence.

"Build a fire, Silva," Wooston said. "Might as well have coffee while we wait."

"You are not afraid they will run again?" Fernandez asked.

Wooston scoffed. "Let them run. We'll find them."

After a moment he added, "I've a hunch this is it. I think the gold is somewhere near."

"Where are we, anyway?" Russell asked.

"Who cares? When we finish with them we will go back. The trail we followed is always there."

From high in the rocks, there was laughter. It sounded like nothing they had ever heard, but it was laughter.

Was the tone as wild and eerie as it sounded? Or was it the echo from the rocks? The wildness of the area and their own imaginations?

Russell hunched his shoulders a little and glanced at the others. Wooston was chewing on some dried beef and Machado was lighting a thin cigar. Tomas looked at Russell and smiled inwardly. The big, tough American was a little frightened, he thought. Look at Machado, a man of iron.

The fire blazed up and they all felt better. "We'll get them tomorrow," Wooston said, "and they'll have some gold."

Back at the clearing Sean went down from the rocks to where Mariana waited. "You were right on time," he said. "It helped."

"So were the others," she said, "but where are they?"

There was no sound. Then Jesus Montero came in to join them. "Put on the pot," he said, "we will have coffee."

"But the Señora!" Mariana said. "I heard them. They should be here!"

"You heard something, Señorita," Montero said. "Who knows what you heard?"

"When I was a little boy," Sean said, "the vaqueros told strange stories about Juan. The Indians went to him whenever anyone was very sick. Sometimes the Californios also."

"He cured them?"

"He did."

Sean stirred the fire and added a few sticks. "Once there were two very bad men who decided to follow him to find the gold they heard about. They were going to force the secret from him."

"What happened?"

"Nobody ever knew. The two men were found dead, no marks on their bodies. Their guns had been fired and not reloaded."

They sipped their coffee and chewed on cold tortillas and dried beef.

"It grows light," Montero said. "We should move now."

"What about the Señora and Juan?" Sean asked.

"They will find us."

Each filled a cup, then Montero poured the coffee on the coals and dipped the pot in the creek to cool it off. He had turned and started back when he suddenly dropped to the ground in a long running dive. A bullet clipped a rock above his head.

Sean, catching up his Colt rifle, ran to the rocks. He caught a shadow of movement, lifted his rifle, and shot. Somebody swore, but it was not the curse of a man wounded.

Under his covering fire Montero made it into the trees. Sean watched him go, and wondered. Wooston and Machado and the others could edge in, could make the place impossible to defend. He reloaded his rifle, waited a bit, then edged away to a new position.

Montero eased up among the rocks. "The horses are ready, amigo. We will go nearer to where the Señora is."

"All right." He fired at a rock where he thought a man was hiding, ran a few steps back, and fired again.

Sliding down from the rocks, he mounted and they

rode their horses up a narrow draw behind the trees. For several hundred yards it was so narrow a man might have almost touched both walls, and it was a scramble for the horses over slick rocks and around boulders. Then they went up a bank and into a small forest of juniper and manzanita. A few minutes later they were in the pines that covered most of the mountain.

Montero led them at a rapid pace along a winding forest trail that took them ever higher upon the pine-clad slopes, often broken by arroyos or canyons.

Topping out on a high ridge, Montero pointed. "The Sespe is there. If anything happens to me, just ride south."

Eileen Mulkerin drew up and looked around her. She was on the south bank of a stream that ran roughly east and west. The creek then turned to flow almost due north. On her left and somewhat higher up there seemed to be a break in the mountain.

Juan had paused only for a moment, and now he turned toward the south, seeming to head toward the break. Several times he doubled back on his trail to wipe it out. He would ride back, get down and ever so gently brush out the tracks with an evergreen bough. Then he would sift dust and pine needles over the brushed-out tracks.

Suddenly he came to a place under a huge old oak that was marked by fallen stones which seemed to have once been a wall. "The horses must stay here. We will walk."

She took her rifle and a water sack, and he led the way, moving with surprising speed among the rocks. He went up the mountain away from the creek. The yucca, which had been plentiful at lower levels, was scarce now. Once, with high, rocky walls rising on both sides, but at least a half mile apart, Juan paused in the shade. "I am afraid there is very little gold." His eyes searched her face. "Perhaps it will not be enough?"

The thought was frightening. She had hoped so much for this.

The idea that there might be no gold, now when they so desperately needed it, was shattering.

"Where does it come from? The gold, I mean?"

Juan paused, then stopped walking, and then answered. "Long ago my people came to this place. It was as far away for us as for you, but we came. And there was some gold here. We had little need for it, and used it for decoration. When our city was destroyed in the earthquakes, we no longer went for the gold."

How had the Mulkerins come to think of it as a treasure? She could not recall that Jaime had ever said anything about quantity, yet somehow it had grown in size with each telling. It was probably the same with all stories of treasure.

All she could do now was hope that there was enough gold remaining to pay what they owed on the ranch.

When they stopped again she looked around. They were in a giant horseshoe almost a mile from the opening to the towering back wall. On three sides the walls went at least a thousand feet above the creek. A skilled mountain climber might climb out, she supposed, but otherwise there would be nothing to do but return the way they had come.

At the head of the creek the rock wall was a massive rampart shutting out most of the light and leaving the great hollow in deep shadow.

"It is here," Juan said. "I will show you."

Near the head of the creek were the scattered rocks of an old structure of some sort. There was a gap in the rocks and a hard-packed path of sand led between them. Juan led the way.

There was a cave there . . . did she see the signs of tools upon the rock walls? And at the end of the cave, a shelf. Upon the shelf was a row of jars. Juan took down one of them, and her heart missed a beat.

She took the jar. There was gold, all right. Gold dust and a few small nuggets, half the size of her little fingernail.

She took the leather pouch she had brought and poured the gold into it.

When she had emptied every grain she hefted it in her hand. Five pounds? It might be . . . but less than half of what was needed.

One after another she checked the other jars. Out of one she took perhaps an ounce. The others were empty.

Juan watched her face anxiously. "It is not enough?"

"It will help," she said, "but it is not enough. But thank you, old friend, you have done all you could. Thank you, thank you!"

All of the years since she first came to California she seemed to have heard stories about this place, and now she was here. Slowly, Eileen Mulkerin looked around.

"We should rest," Juan suggested. "It is a long way back."

"They will be waiting," Eileen Mulkerin said, "and they may be in trouble."

"Jesus Montero will know what to do," Juan said. "We must rest, Señora. We must rest here."

Chapter 11

Within the cave it was cool and silent. The old man sat down against the wall and leaned his head back, sighing deeply. Despite her fear, Eileen Mulkerin was shocked to see the terrible weariness in the old man's face.

She had been so filled with her own troubles that she had not considered the great strain this journey must have been for him. She was tired, and she was one who rode or walked every day, who had been in the saddle since she was a child, and since coming to California had ridden over the roughest, wildest country imaginable.

"Rest, Old One," she said gently. "I have been thoughtless."

"I shall rest," he replied, "but you rest, also. And . . ." he opened his eyes and looked at her, "do not go from this place. There is great danger here . . . the greatest."

He leaned his head back again and closed his eyes, but there was to be no sleep for her, not yet.

What could he mean by great danger here? She stood in the mouth of the cave looking about her.

The horseshoe curve of mountains was bare rock in places, covered with pines in others, but all around her the cliffs rose high.

The stillness was oppressive. She listened for sound. Somewhere, not too many miles away, Sean might now be fighting for his life. He was shrewd, tough, a good fighter. Montero was, too, old though he might be. The girl Mariana, there was good stuff there. She had taken the long ride without complaint, had done whatever she could to make things easier. That she came from a good home as well as a wealthy one was obvious. She had the knowledge and the deportment that went with such things.

Was Sean in love with her? It would not be surprising, she thought, for Mariana was certainly beautiful, and a man's woman. No question of that.

The silence seemed to press in on her. Why had Juan said the place was dangerous? She saw nothing of danger.

High up on the rim, she saw something move. No doubt the wind, she supposed.

More than anything she needed time to think. The shock of that almost empty jar had been just about more than she could bear.

They had been so sure the gold was there and that it would be enough, so much so that when doubts were raised they had never accepted them as possible. In their minds this had been a source where there would always be a little, just enough, to tide them over.

Now they would lose everything, all the land Jaime had hoped to leave to his sons, the land Mexico had given for his service as an officer in their army. All that she had wanted for her boys, now gone.

She felt sick and empty. It could not be, it simply could not be. Yet the facts were remorseless, relentless.

She refused to accept defeat. There had to be a way. She was alive, she was strong, she had intelligence. She had simply trusted too much to this place, in this gold gathered by unknown hands so long, long ago.

They had come far for it, Juan had said. As far as she herself had come. Yet where had the gold itself come from? Had it been mined close by? The cave did not appear mineralized, the rocks seemed barren.

There were tool marks on the stone at the entrance,

which seemed to have been enlarged, and even the cave itself had been shaped to some degree.

Why?

The gold itself did not look like placer gold, but of course, it would not, if it had been gathered here. The source of the gold itself must be near, for the small nuggets were jagged, rough, showing none of the signs of abrasion from being rolled among the rocks and gravel of a rushing stream.

The source? It might be some corner, some hollow nearby, and it might be anywhere up in those towering cliffs around her. If they only had the time—

But they had no time.

Even the stone and gravel ledge upon which she stood, which opened out at the cave's mouth to make a flat, even surface to the creek's bank, seemed to have been leveled and smoothed for some purpose.

Evidently they had come here, as Juan said, from some distance, and had remained in this place until they had sufficient gold for their purpose.

Yet where had it come from? She had seen no evidence of mining, nor of any work whatsoever, merely this cave, not very impressive of itself, and this terrace on the creek bank.

From the terrace before the cave she could see nothing of the country around except the high walls of the horseshoe cliffs, trees, brush, and boulders intervening. It was an eerie, haunted place. Uneasily she walked across the terrace and looked down the stream bed.

She could see only a little way, but the water dropped swiftly. It was not a cheerful stream, but one that ran swift and dark under the shadows of cliff and tree. She poked at the sand under the clear water. Could there be gold there?

Suddenly, from far off, there was a call. It was a

lonely call, seemingly undirected, as lonely as a wolf calling to the moon. She shivered.

Should she awaken Juan? The old man had seemed frighteningly tired, and after all, it had been only a few minutes ago that he fell asleep.

She was being a fool. What was there to be afraid of? Not one chance in a thousand that anyone could find her here in this cul-de-sac. It was an unlikely place to come, for there was so obviously no place to go but back.

"Jaime," she spoke softly. "I need you, Jaime."

The leaves rustled, and there was stillness. She lifted her eyes toward the cliffs. They seemed to shimmer in the heat, but she felt suddenly cold as though a chill wind had blown down the canyon. But there was no wind.

Again she heard that strange, lonely cry. She could not place the direction. It seemed to come from far off, from no place in particular.

She remembered the stories about Juan, the way the other Indians avoided talking about him. Even Jesus Montero, who knew her so well, would not talk about him. They spoke of him as having strange powers, of disappearing into broad daylight. Indians were superstitious and believed in all manner of things.

Suppose they were right? She remembered one night by the fireside back at the ranch when Jaime had suddenly begun talking to her of an old medicine man he had known in Mexico. They had come upon him injured by the roadside, looking as though he had fallen, yet there was no place to fall from. They had taken him with them, fed him, cared for him, treated his wounds. He recovered miraculously but to Jaime, when they were alone, he told a strange story. He had, he said, been traveling on the "other side."

98

When asked about the other side he had been evasive and would say only that it looked like this but was different, that he had often been to the other side but this time there was "trouble" and he could not find his way back, and when he saw a "sipapu" it was not where he had expected. It was one unknown to him, and he had fallen.

"I think," Jaime had said, "that wherever the other side is, Juan has been there, too."

"But what does it mean?"

He had shrugged. "How can I say? The people of America were not all savages, you know. At Monte Alban in Mexico I saw observatories for studying the stars far better than anything we have. How do we know what they knew?"

She remembered a padre at San Gabriel Mission had told her of the belief the Hopis had, of coming to this earth from a "hole in the ground" and that place had been called a "sipapu," or something of that sort.

She had asked Jaime what the old medicine man had meant when he found his sipapu where it was not expected to be.

"All I could get from him were that there were certain places, some of them constant, some shifting in position, where one might pass through the curtain to the other side. In seeking the one he knew, he found one of which he had known nothing."

It would grow dark quickly in this place, for the cliffs would allow only sunlight from overhead. She looked around, then walked back to the cave. Glancing through the door she saw the old man stretched upon the floor.

She would wait a little longer. Seated by the door, she thought of possible solutions, one by one. Even those she discarded, she examined once again.

Alvarado was their friend and had been her husband's friend, but he was far away to the north. Pio, although he was a kindly man, had troubles of his own.

Their debts were not large, scarcely twenty-five hundred dollars in all, but that was a large sum in California in these times. Not long ago a ranch as large as their own had sold for even less, and they had no friend who could come up with so much.

Only there was a difference. They now had almost half the sum. Could they somehow come up with the rest? They might sell the *Lady Luck*, but it would bring very little now, and the governor was growing harsher about inspecting cargoes.

They still had several hundred hides, but unless an unexpected trading vessel showed up, there was no market for them. They had not traded furs since Sean's voyage. They had cattle and horses but so did everybody else and there was simply no market for them.

Again and again she went over the ground, taking each item in turn.

It was very hot, and the late afternoon sun struck directly upon her. Heat waves shimmered, even more than on the desert. She got up, feeling a little nausea, and for a moment thought she saw an Indian standing at the edge of the terrace. She started to speak, moved forward, and then the illusion faded and there was only the heat waves above a bare place on the rocky ledge beyond the terrace.

It was time to go. Juan might be tired, but she must awaken him. Turning, she went to the cave. Her head ached, and she was worried and frightened, yet her sense of fear seemed to have no focal point, only an all-pervading feeling of strangeness and uncertainty.

The old man lay upon the floor. Apparently he had not moved.

"Juan? We must go. There will be trouble."

The old man did not move, nor did he speak. Suddenly shocked, she stepped into the cave and bent over him.

"Juan? *Juan!*"

There was no answer. She touched him, shook him slightly. He did not move. His eyes were open, staring upward at the cave roof.

He was dead.

She touched his eyes gently, closing them. His skin was cool to the touch. He must have died shortly after lying down.

She took up the jacket she had worn when they first came up the creek and placed it over him.

"Sleep, Juan," she said gently. "You have earned it."

She took her rifle and canteen and left the cave, turning toward the faint path along the creek. She walked swiftly to where their horses were resting.

Nothing was to be gained here. She had what gold there was, and she felt sure Juan's body would be safe in the cave. She had seen no animal tracks about, nor had she seen even a lizard or a bird. Later, they could come back and bury the old man, but for now there was nothing she could do.

Untying the horses, she mounted quickly, and, leading Juan's horse, started down the trail, riding swiftly.

Now she had but one driving thought. Get back to the others, stand with them, and when they could, slip away and return to the Malibu. The answer, she felt sure, was there and not here.

She had ridden for almost an hour before she heard a sound other than those of her own movements. When she heard it, the sound came from far off. It was a rifle shot.

Pointing her rifle at the sky, she fired.

Maybe they would hear that and know she was coming, or maybe the others would hear it and wonder who it might be. Murder is not lightly done and even Machado, with his reckless disregard for law, would hesitate. So would Wooston, essentially a cautious man. Probably they had no idea that she was not with Sean, or that the party had been divided.

She rode at a rapid trot, the best pace for the ground she covered, and she kept her rifle ready.

Suddenly, long before she expected to come up with them, she heard another shot.

Rounding a bend in the trail, she pulled up short. They were just before her, almost opposite the head of the Piedra Blanca, with Mariana leading the pack-horses and Montero and Sean coming along slower.

Montero saw her and rode up swiftly. "We have a little time, Señora, but we must go back."

"Do you remember the old trail? Back of Reyes Peak?"

"Sí, Señora. It has been years, but—"

"Lead us then. Somewhere we should be able to cut over to the Cherry Creek trail to Old Man Canyon. We will go home now. Lose them if you can."

Sean rode swiftly up, glancing suddenly at the empty saddle of the lead horse.

"Juan?"

"He is dead. He died back there after he showed me the gold."

"I am sorry. He was a fine old man, a fine man. I could have learned much from him."

"He told me he had taught you what was most important. He said it would not seem like much, but it was, and you would see."

"Let's go. We've killed nobody yet and I'd prefer not to."

"Sean? There isn't enough. There is scarcely half enough."

He shot her a quick glance, then nodded. "I was afraid. I suspected."

"We must think of something, Sean. We must think quickly, you and me."

"Did you see where the gold came from? Any old workings?"

"No. It was a strange, empty place. The gold was in a pot on a shelf, most of the other pots were empty. The Old One wanted to rest and he lay down in the cave. He must have died almost at once but I did not know it for several hours."

They rode on, turning sharply south for about a mile, then west again with Reyes Peak bulking large on their left and ahead.

"Sean, there's something strange about that place. I was almost sick up there, dizzy. Once I thought I saw an Indian of some kind, but he just faded out."

" 'Of some kind'? What kind?"

"He was . . . different, I guess. I just caught a glimpse, but it was my imagination, anyway."

Sean glanced back. Could he see dust in the air? Or was that, too, imagination?

Nothing his mother had said surprised him . . . why? He turned the thought in his mind, puzzled by it.

He prided himself on being a straightforward, hard-headed man of the sea . . . of the sea? Did that make a difference? For the men who sail upon the deep water see too much of the unbelievable and mysterious, they travel to faraway lands where customs, religions, and thoughts are all keyed to a different tempo, and somewhere along the line become less resistant to the amazing, the unusual, and the seemingly unreasonable.

Or was it simply the Irish in him? That Celtic background of Druids and leprechauns? Of chieftains, saints, and pagan gods?

The top of Reyes Peak was lit by the fire of sunset, and a soft wind from the sea moved through the pines. Suddenly they emerged from the trees riding along the ridge of Pine Mountain toward the west.

Eileen Mulkerin stood in her stirrups, her hair blowing in the wind, and looked back the way they had come. "I hope they can ride!" she commented grimly. "Before they see their homes again they'll have been around!"

Montero slowed his pace. Along the skyline they went, Montero leading, followed by Mariana and the pack animals, then Eileen Mulkerin and Sean.

She glanced at him. "That girl of yours is strong stuff," she said, "not a word of complaint from her and she does what she can and stays out of the way."

He smiled. "She's not mine, Señora, although—"

"I know," Eileen Mulkerin looked again at the slender girl ahead of them, "but she's made of good yardage, that one. She will stay with you, all the way."

"Yes, I think so."

The trail suddenly veered to the right over a rocky surface, but Jesus did not turn. He pushed right on, going between close-growing pines, turning abruptly down a steep slide, and picking his way along the side of a boulder-strewn canyon into a thick stand of timber.

The trees were old, yet few were over thirty or forty feet tall, and there was evidence that a fire had swept through. Their way was steeply down through chaparral and yucca, the slopes dry and harsh.

When the pace slowed, and the shadows lengthened, Sean rode up beside his mother.

"Have you thought of what we will do?" he asked.

"I have thought. We will give a fandango!"

He stared at her. "You are joking?"

"No, a fandango. It is the answer. We will invite them all! Our friends, our enemies . . . everyone!"

She laughed at his amazement. "We do not have the money, right? But we have some money, and do they know how much? They do not! They will see some gold, and their imaginations will make it three times as much! We will laugh at them. We will taunt them with our splendor.

"They will never believe this gold is all! So we shall show a little of it, let their imaginations believe there is much more, and privately we will tell a few that there can be more . . . and indeed there can . . . but it takes money. First, this trifling debt . . . it must be paid. And *then!*"

He shook his head. "Only you would have the nerve, the audacity . . . !"

"It will work," she said quietly. "We shall win not by what there is, but by what they believe there is."

Chapter 12

Montero lagged behind, brushing lightly over their trail, then sifting dust over it to erase any marks that might be left. He held the dust high and let the breeze carry it where it would.

Sean took the lead, with the Señora behind him. Occasionally, they rode side by side. He was a strong man, this son of hers, she decided. A man fit to move large upon the land. He was quiet, but very sure, and his trail sense was excellent.

They found their way over the Cherry Creek trail

to the Upper North Fork of Matilija Creek. About a half mile further along, Sean turned into a cove among the rocks and rode back into a corner of the cliffs. There, obscured by live oaks and several huge old sycamores, was a level place. Blackened stones showed where others had camped, long ago.

Stepping down from the saddle, he offered his hand to his mother, then to Mariana.

"You knew this place?" Mariana suggested.

"No, but I could see the setback in the cliff face, and knew there were such places." He stripped the saddle from her horse.

Sean let the horses roll, then picketed them on a patch of grass nearby. There was a little water in the creek and their picket ropes allowed them to drink.

Montero rode in a few minutes later and began putting a fire together. "It is safe," he said. "They will not find us tonight."

Eileen Mulkerin did not sit down. She stood, feet apart, looking into the small flame. She liked the smell of the crushed juniper, the smell of wood-smoke, and the soft rustling of the water in the creek.

Many times in the past she had camped in just such places with Jaime, and she was thinking of him now, of his lean, strong body, the ease with which he moved, the grace of him.

She rarely thought of him as dead. She liked to believe he was only away, that he would come back to her one day, and in the meanwhile she must do the best she could to preserve what belonged to them.

If they could get back with the little gold they had, if they could ride into the pueblo of Los Angeles and buy things with some of this gold, people would start to talk, and she would be able to hold off Zeke Wooston and Fernandez.

Gold was rarely seen and the sight of it would revive the old stories. If she said she would pay soon, the Californios would believe her, and Wooston would hesitate to push too hard.

The fandango would be a bold stroke, a show of confidence that would add to the belief that she had enough or would soon have enough to pay.

A bat dipped and swirled in the air above them, and not far off a mockingbird was singing his endless songs into the night stillness.

She gathered wood, and Montero broiled beef over the fire. They sat together, talking very little, enjoying the night, the rest, and the food as well as the smell of wood-smoke and coffee.

Sean took up his Colt rifle and moved away from the fire, but after a few minutes he was back. "Seems quiet enough," he said.

Jesus Montero glanced up at him, then at the Señora. "The Old One is dead," he said softly. "It is not easy to believe."

"We must go back and bury him when there is time," Sean suggested.

"What about his body?" Eileen asked. "Will it be safe from wolves?"

Montero did not look up from his food but he said distinctly, "No animal will go where he lies."

Sean looked at him. "You mean wherever he lies . . . or where he lies now?"

"Did you see animals there? Or birds?"

"No," she said reluctantly, "I did not."

"His body will be safe," Montero replied. "It is not a thing for worry."

"There will be Machado to deal with," Sean commented. "He will make trouble."

"Leave him to me," Eileen replied quietly. "It is all

107

different now. We have a show of gold, and our position is stronger. You will see. It will make a difference, and Mariana shall help me plan the fandango." She smiled. "We shall even invite Andres Machado. We shall invite them all!"

"They are gone," Silva said. "Disappeared."

"That's foolishness!" Wooston said impatiently. "They came this way, they moved about, they left. There must be tracks."

"I think," Fernandez interrupted, "the gold is nearby. I think they stopped here, some went away for the gold and the others stayed."

"Let's find the gold then," Wooston said. "To hell with them."

"I do not care for gold," Machado said. "I want them. I will kill them. All of them."

"You go ahead an' kill 'em," Russell said, "we'll hunt for the gold."

Silva was silent. He glanced at the other vaqueros and the one called Francisco shrugged expressively.

"You will not find the gold," Silva said. "Only the Old One knows."

Wooston glanced at him irritably. Then he said, "We hired you for a tracker. Find 'em."

Wooston walked over to the remains of the fire. It was cold and dead. How could they have slipped away like that? He stared around the rocky cliffs, then slowly walked along the edge of the brush. He could see where the horses had been held, where the various people had slept, yet there seemed to be no tracks leading from the place.

Zeke Wooston was a hard, bitter man, a greedy man and a cruel one. From boyhood, when he had been a hulking bully in a class of younger children, all of whom had been quicker and brighter than he, he had relied on strength rather than intelligence. But over the years he had developed a kind of cunning, and a grasp of character that was shrewd and penetrating.

He knew very well whom he could frighten, knew those with whom he must be genial, and those to avoid. Ordinarily he would have avoided Sean Mulkerin. As for the widow Mulkerin, she was nothing but a woman for all their talk and he was not worried about her. She'd scare . . . they all did.

He wanted money and he wanted power. King-Pin Russell, a vindictive, dangerous man, was a tool to that end. Russell was a man who if offered two ways would always choose the dishonest one. It was his nature. He was tough and egotistical, sure of his own shrewdness, and with nothing but contempt for honest men. They were suckers, he said, they were incompetent fools.

Why most of them lived better, easier, and with freedom from his pressures had never occurred to him. He was sure most of them were secretly stealing or would have if they had the nerve.

Basically Russell was a follower. First it was one man, then another. Now it was Wooston, whom he disliked but who always seemed to have money. He lived easier in Wooston's shadow, and did what he was told until he could make a big strike himself and come away with enough money to tell them all to go to hell.

From the moment he had first heard of the gold he had determined to have it for himself. Nobody in California had found any gold but there were rumors of it, and the Spanish had found gold in Mexico. Why shouldn't there be some here?

It was obvious the gold's source was nearby. Why else had they stopped here?

He watched Wooston prowling about, studying the rocks, the tracks, the country around. Zeke thought it was here, too, or close by. Machado did not care. All he wanted was a knife in Sean's ribs and a whip for that girl.

Fernandez wanted gold, but he wanted it quick and easy, the kind you could dig with a knife . . . from somebody's ribs.

Tomas? Tomas would bear watching. He was quieter, said less, watched more, and was steadier than any of the rest.

Russell took the stub of a cigar from his pocket and lit it. His eyes strayed to Francisco. Aside from Silva he was the best tracker in the lot, and a wary, careful man as well. Francisco glanced his way and King-Pin offered him a cigar.

Francisco was no fool. The American or Englishman or whatever he was wanted something. Well, so did he.

He took the cigar. "Gracias," he said, with a flash of white, even teeth. "Señor is generous."

"No, I ain't," Russell replied shortly. "But I've been noticing you're an almighty fine tracker . . . maybe better than Silva."

Francisco shrugged.

"Seems to me that gold is somewhere around. Now if you was to see anything, some little thing nobody else saw, you could tell me.

"Wooston is impatient. So is Machado. They will want to move on, but you an' me . . . we might sort of fall back. Then we could look around a mite . . . say we got lost?"

Francisco lit the cigar. His black eyes were steady. He knew when he was about to be used, but Russell was a dangerous man, and in difficulty could be useful.

"Silva," he suggested, "does not tell all. Silva is

110

afraid of the Old One . . . many are. The Old One left the others here and went into the hills with the Señora. We have seen their tracks."

"You could follow them?"

Francisco shrugged. "Who knows? It is not easy to follow the Old One." He looked at his cigar, then said, "Nor is it safe, Señor."

Russell dismissed that with a gesture. "You an' me, we'll fall back, get lost. All right?"

"All right." Francisco drew deep on his cigar. He did not like this King-Pin, but if there was gold . . . enough of it . . . well, a knife in the ribs before King-Pin could shoot him, which he was sure Russell would try to do when the gold was found.

Zeke Wooston walked back to the fire which Russell had rekindled. "Ain't no time for that," he said impatiently. "We got to ride out."

"There is no trail," Silva said. "There is only rock, and around this camp there are many tracks, tracks coming, going . . . but none of them go anywhere."

"I think he does not want to follow the trail," Andres Machado said. "He is a coward."

Silva did not reply. He had learned the folly of talking back to men like Machado. It was not a thing to do if one wished to live long, and he, Silva, had lived long and expected to live longer.

"The Old One," he said after a moment, trying to choose his words, "follows trails we cannot. All trails are not of this world, Señor."

Wooston grunted. "I reckon we can foller any trail he can foller. He an' that Señora woman."

Silva glanced at him quickly. "Ah?"

"Yes, I seen 'em. I ain't no tracker like some of these here Injuns, but I can read signs. The two of them taken off . . . now where do you suppose?"

"Follow them, Señor," Silva suggested, delicately.

111

"Your eyes are younger than mine, sharper, perhaps. Follow them. I cannot."

"You mean you won't?"

"I shall follow the others."

"You mean they went separately?"

"They are not here, Señor. They are gone." He waited for a minute and then said quietly, "I think they have gone back. I think they found what they wanted and they have gone back."

Andres Machado frowned. Why waste time in these godforsaken mountains if they were not here? If they had gone back—

"You are sure of that?"

Silva shrugged. "Who can be sure? It is what I believe."

"That settles it for me." Machado was definite. He was bored with mountains, bored with camping, irritated by the poor food, and the heat, dust, and confusion. He was also bored by Wooston. The man was coarse and vulgar.

"We ain't found where they get that gold," Wooston protested. "It has got to be close by."

Machado shrugged a shoulder. "Perhaps. I am not interested in the 'gold' if gold there is. I am sufficiently well-off, Señor Wooston. I came only to find Mulkerin and Mariana de la Cruz. I shall go back, and I shall take my men with me."

"Now see here!" Wooston protested. "We started this together, an'—"

"And now it is ended. If Mulkerin has returned to Malibu, I shall return also. I see no sense in running around over these awful hills looking for gold that may not even be here.

"Gold in California? Bah! There is none. My family has been associated with this province from the beginning, and we know nothing of any gold. You pursue a will-o'-the-wisp, my friend."

Wooston was angry, but he had no wish to have trouble with Machado, whom he might need very badly. But he did not wish to pursue a chase into this wild country with only his own group. There were too few of them.

Wooston accepted a cup of coffee, mulling over the situation. He had no liking for this kind of country himself. It gave him the willies . . . you could never tell who or what was back in that brush or behind the rocks. And what about that snake that wasn't there? What about those strange howls from up in the rocks?

"All right," he said, "we'll go back."

Francisco glanced at King-Pin Russell, who grinned and winked.

Chapter 13

Eileen Mulkerin rode into the yard at the ranch on Malibu with her son beside her. Behind them were Mariana and Jesus Montero.

She drew up in the yard and looked at the rough-looking crowd who faced her. Renegades, all of them, some gringos, some Mexicans.

Brother Michael sat on the porch in the shade. He had a rifle across his knees.

She looked at the renegades with eyes that were cold and level. "You have no business here. You will leave."

Their leader, a swaggering man in a wide sombrero and wide-bottomed pants, wearing two guns, laughed. "I am Greek John," he said, sneering. "I do not go when a woman speaks. Señor Wooston told me to stay until he comes. I stay."

"My mother told you to leave," Sean said quietly. "You have one minute."

Greek John was lean, whip-hard, and strong. He touched his mustache lightly and smiled. "Come, little one," he said, "I shall teach you."

Sean dismounted from his horse and trailed the reins. "Señora?" he spoke gently. "Forgive me."

He swung, his fist exploding on the Greek's chin. The Greek dropped to hands and knees, his sombrero flying loose. For a moment he stayed there, shaking his head. When he got up he held a knife in his hand.

"Now I shall kill you," he said.

Sean made no move toward the Bowie, nor the Paterson Colt .36 on his hip. He simply waited.

The Greek came forward, the knife low. Sean measured him with expertise gained on the waterfronts of Shanghai, Singapore, Amurang, and Taku Bar. The man moved well, held his knife low, cutting edge up.

The man came on, the knife in his right hand. He would thrust and cut to the left, Sean was sure. Hands ready, he waited. The Greek suddenly feinted, lunged, and thrust. Sean side-stepped quickly to the left and saw the blade sweep to his right, and then Sean slashed at the Greek's ear with the edge of his hand.

It was a chopping, backward blow that landed solidly and staggered the Greek. He missed a step, and Sean turned quickly. Dazed, the Greek was almost as quick. Sean feinted, the Greek thrust wildly, and Sean hit him solidly on the chin with a right.

The Greek's knees folded and Sean stepped in and kicked him on the chin. The knife went flying, and the Greek hit the dust and fell back.

Sean walked calmly to him, jerked him half erect

and hit him once in the solar plexus, hooking the punch with vicious force. Then dragging him by the scruff of the neck he took him to a saddled horse, obviously belonging to one of the invaders. "Take him, and get out."

It was cool and quiet inside the adobe ranch house. Eileen Mulkerin paused in the living room and looked slowly around. Nothing had changed, this was her home. It was familiar, bare by some standards, but it was home and she loved every inch of it.

"Did you have trouble, Michael?"

"No. They didn't quite know what to do about me." He smiled. "There is an advantage in being of the Church, Señora. I just sat and they let me be after a few minutes of argument."

He got to his feet. "I must go now. I have duties."

"Of course, but will you tell everyone there is to be a fandango here, a week from Friday?"

Michael glanced at her. His mother never surprised him anymore. "A fandango? Of course."

When he had gone she turned to Mariana. "Come. You can help me."

Sean Mulkerin walked outside, squinting his eyes against the glare of the sun on the hard-packed clay of the yard. Heat waves shimmered, and he glanced toward the corral, then the hills around.

His mother's strategy was good, of course. Nobody would dream they did not have the money. She would spend a little of the gold, say nothing, and let them imagine how much she had. Wooston would probably demand immediate payment, but he would get little sympathy from the Californios who would now be sure she had the money and would permit him to take no action. Sean knew from past experience how they thought. They would simply say, "You know she has the money. When she is ready, she will pay. Do nothing."

Sean Mulkerin climbed the low mountain near the ranch and looked toward the sea. The *Lady Luck* was anchored now in Paradise Cove. Tennison had shifted the schooner to have it closer in case of need.

Sean checked his gun again. Despite his mother's reassurances, he was worried. Zeke Wooston was not like the men she had known, and he might not be susceptible to public pressure.

They had lost him back in the hills but he would return and the men he had with him were not the kind to be easily turned from their purpose. They wanted the Malibu, and they would try by every means to get it.

Montero was braiding a rawhide riata when he walked back down the footpath to the adobe.

"We're going to need a couple of hands," he said quietly, "men we can trust."

Montero nodded. "I have them. They are coming."

"You've already sent for them?"

"Before you returned I knew they would be needed. These are good men, tough men."

"When will they be here?"

"Today, tomorrow . . . who knows? They are coming."

The Señora would be riding to the pueblo, to Los Angeles. It was the thing to do now, to go in, to spend gold, to invite all to the fandango, the families of Sepulveda, Lugo, Verdugo, Abel Stearns . . . all of them.

In the meantime, life must go on, and Sean had to plan for the future of the ranch. Ground must be plowed, crops seeded. Many of the Californios were content to live as they always had, their cattle running wild upon thousands of acres, growing their few crops,

116

existing in a pleasant sort of never-never land where all was peace and contentment and nobody had to struggle too much.

That was the trouble with California in the 1840's. The life was too easy, there was no necessity for struggle, and men must struggle or they deteriorate.

His thoughts returned to the gold. If they had come to that area for gold, then the gold must have been washed from the stream close to its point of origin, or dry-washed from the slides. The Señora had said there was no evidence of mining close by, although the cave itself showed some signs of work, very ancient work. Scowling he walked to the end of the porch and stood there, leaning against the pole at the corner.

There was no other way. He must go back. He must find the place to which Juan had taken his mother, bury Juan's body, and look for the gold.

In the meantime he must start things moving here in a more practical way. Men had spent their lives looking for lost mines or treasures and found nothing. He would not take that route. First he would set the wheels in motion.

There were several thousand head of cattle on the Malibu. If he could round up all over six years old, get the hides and tallow, he would have a beginning. Besides, he had an idea of getting a bull from the Mormons at San Bernardino. He had seen their cattle, all bigger, fatter, and better than the cattle he had. With a bull or two he could breed his own herd, for while beef was a drug on the market now, it might not always be. In the meanwhile there was some seed left from their planting venture. They could try that.

He would ride up the coast and talk to the Chumash. They had rarely come to the ranch since his father died, but it was a contact that must not be lost. Through

117

them he might establish connections with Indians from the interior who had furs to trade.

There was no time to waste.

"Jesus," he said, as Montero approached the porch, "let the word get around that we will trade for furs. I want to reach the mountain Indians."

Montero said, "I think this is good."

He paused. "Capitan, two men have come. They are not strangers to me although I have not seen them before."

"What sort of men?"

"Vaqueros, Capitan. They are good men with the horse, the cow, the riata." He paused again. "They are also good men for the fight."

"Where do they come from?"

"Sonora, Capitan. At least, that was the last place, but one of them was once in the army with your father."

"I will see them."

An hour later they rode up to the ranch. They came up the trail at full gallop, pulled up before the ranch house, and swung down. Both were obviously magnificent horsemen. The older man, whom Sean immediately knew must be the one who had served with his father, was broad and thick, but with muscle, not fat.

"Cabeza Del Campo," he said, introducing himself, a sly glint in his eye. "I was a sergeant with your father, Señor. Four years I rode with him, from the time I was sixteen until I was twenty."

"Since then?"

His eyes twinkled. "I have lived, Señor."

Sean turned his attention to the younger man, scarcely more than a boy. He was lean and hard, showing more Indian than Spanish.

"Antonio Polanco, Señor. I would serve you."

"It is hard work here," Sean told them, "and there

may be fighting. Loyalty is of first importance. When you no longer wish to work here, come to me and speak. You can go then."

"It is understood."

"Our enemies outnumber us. They are shrewd and intelligent. We want no violence, but if you are attacked or the people here or the place are endangered, fight. If you fight, win. If the odds are too great get out gracefully if you can. There is always another day."

"Sí Señor. It is understood."

He glanced from one to the other. "My mother is in command here. After her there is me, and after me, Jesus Montero. It is understood?"

"It is."

Sean looked at them again, then turned to Montero. "Do not look for other men. I think these two will be enough."

Del Campo glanced at Polanco. "Did you hear that, amigo?" he spoke softly. "He says we are enough. So it must be."

In the rough country east of Pine Mountain, Zeke Wooston and his group twice lost their way. Disgruntled and irritated they finally made camp only a few miles from their starting point.

"You was supposed to be a tracker," Wooston said irritably to Silva.

"A tracker, Señor, but not a man who knows this country. You wished to go back by a shorter way, it is a way that is strange to me. In the morning—"

"In the morning I will lead us out," Wooston declared. "Where's King-Pin?"

Silva shrugged. None of the others knew either. "Francisco is with him," somebody said. "They turned into a wrong canyon, perhaps."

Wooston was not pleased. He wanted his men together. No telling what they might run into. The long trek through the mountains and their failure to follow the widow and her son had angered him. There was too much delay. He had cargoes coming in within the week and he wanted no trouble with anyone when they landed on the coast. He had already advised them that the Malibu would be his, that they could come in safely at that point.

Suddenly a fierce anger rose within him. He was a man who could not abide frustration, and this damned Irish woman and her cub had—

"Beltran!"

Beltran was a man he had watched closely. Although Beltran did not know it, Wooston had checked his background enough to know he was a murderer, had been a bandit, and was wanted by the law at a dozen places in Mexico. He was an excellent shot, good with any weapon, and a fine horseman. He rode with Velasco, and they made a nasty team.

"Señor?"

Wooston looked into Beltran's black eyes and felt a slight chill. The man was as deadly as a rattler. "Take Velasco," he drew two gold eagles from his pocket, "and kill Señora Mulkerin and her son, the captain. Do you understand?"

Beltran shrugged. He fingered the two coins in his hand. "What is this?" he asked softly. "This gold? It is not enough, Señor."

"You will get more when it is done. There will be four more pieces of gold for each if it is done within the week, and if you are caught, it was a robbery you attempted . . . nothing more."

"Sí."

Beltran walked to Velasco. He handed him a gold piece, then explained. "Good! We will do it . . . but carefully, amigo. Very carefully."

"It is not a good thing," Velasco said, "to kill a beautiful woman. Perhaps it would be better if—"

"He said *kill*. It is what we will do, Velasco. We will only kill . . . very quickly. Then we will rob them and there is San Francisco."

"Of course," Velasco said carelessly, but he was thinking his own thoughts.

Chapter 14

In the pueblo of Los Angeles the houses were of adobe, their almost flat roofs plastered with asphalt from the tar pits at Rancho La Brea. There were many trails into the town, most of them old Indian trails that had been found useful.

There was a guardhouse in the town, and a church, a few trading posts and stores, here and there a cantina. A scattering of homes lay along the various roads and streets, and the population was about fourteen hundred, depending on the season or the time of day.

The trail from Malibu to the pueblo lay along the shore for a few miles, then joined with the old Indian trail from the coast, to the tar pits, to the town, usually called El Camino Viejo . . . the old road.

Eileen Mulkerin rode into the dusty street on a black gelding, a high-stepping horse with his neck arched and a fine sense of pride.

She rode with style, a style the Irish have carried with them to many far lands. She rode sidesaddle, her flaring skirt draped effectively, and to see her no man would have dreamed that she had two tall sons, or that the man who rode beside her was one of them.

They turned into the street, her black horse prancing a little and stopped before the door of a trading post.

Sean swung down and offered his hand to his mother, and she stepped down like a princess. The two vaqueros tilted their sombreros and looked about with the confidence of men who know their strength and for whom they ride.

Eileen swept through the door Sean held aside for her and entered the post. She glanced around, smiled at the storekeeper who almost dropped his broom and hastily straightened the leather apron he wore.

"Yes, Señora?"

She placed her order before him. "I will pay," she said quietly, "in gold."

He looked up quickly. There was little coin in California, and less gold. Men paid in hides, tallow, furs, or in whatever they might have to trade.

"Gold?" The merchant was startled.

"In gold," she repeated, dropping the remark carelessly while looking at some fabric on the counter.

She ordered quickly, moving from one counter to the next, wasting no time. She ordered food, wine, dress material, several imported delicacies rarely found in California, and then she paid for it with small nuggets.

"We are entertaining," she said then, "a small fandango. Will you tell our friends? I shall send riders . . . but you know how it is, and someone might be missed."

"Of course, Señora." He swallowed with some difficulty as he gathered the nuggets and weighed them. "I have not seen so much gold since . . . since. . . ."

"My husband was here?" she shrugged a lovely shoulder. "It is difficult . . . the gold, I mean. One does not have it close by, and it is rather a bother.

"I must have more mules," she added, "for the next time."

"Yes, yes of course." There was respect in the merchant's eyes. "Perhaps Don Abel Stearns, or Señor Wolfskill will have mules to sell . . . or loan."

"Oh, yes, they might have." Eileen Mulkerin gathered her skirts. "Will you have this ready? Our cart will be here soon to pick it up."

"Of course! Of course!"

They would all be there, of course, and there were forty or fifty foreigners in the vicinity now. William Wolfskill had been a trapper, now he owned a vast ranch and was growing oranges to ship. Don Benito Wilson, Hugo Reid, Don Juan Temple, William Workman, John Rowland, had also come west and most of them had married daughters of old California families.

Eileen Mulkerin left the store, pausing briefly on the walk outside. Her eyes swept the dusty street. It was a far cry from Dublin or Cork, far different from London and Paris, yet she loved the old adobes where the whitewash was peeling from the bricks, the dogs lay comfortably in the dust, wagging lazy tails at the occasional passing rider.

Three riders came down the street, handsome boys scarcely into their teens, yet already magnificent horsemen. All three were richly dressed, and they bowed to her with decorum and a certain flair that was all their own. Two of them were Sepulvedas, and the third was Antonio Yorba.

She knew she could expect them at the fandango, for they never missed anything of the sort, and people of all ages came, for there were no parties for the young, the middle-aged, or the old. All gathered together, falling into their various groups at times, and mixing at other times.

The Californios were great dancers and they possessed a manner and style like nothing she had seen, even in France or Spain.

"Señora! It is good to see you!"

She turned quickly. Pio Pico was a somewhat portly man, shrewd and kindly, always active in local affairs.

"I have been shopping, Señor. You will come to our fandango?"

"This is the first I had heard. A fandango is it? But of course!"

Even Pio might be fooled by the gold, but he would wish to be fooled, for he had been a friend of Jaime's, and was a friend of hers.

"You have had trouble, Señora?"

"Señor Wooston has a small debt. He wishes to take the ranch! It is absurd, is it not? I shall pay him, of course, but the gold takes time, and at this season there is much to do. It is not," she added glibly, "as if we did not have it. Jaime always found enough to handle such affairs, but Sean has been away, and with Michael in the Church—"

"I understand, Señora. Of course, you will not lose the ranch. Of course not." His eyes twinkled a little. "And what a time for a fandango! Beautiful, Señora! Simply beautiful!"

There was no fooling Pio, of course. Her chin lifted a little and she smiled impudently. "I thought you would approve, Don Pio, and would you please pass the word to all our friends? There will be much to eat, wine to drink, and there will be dancing!"

After a few minutes more, she watched him go up the street, pleased that she had scored a point in her favor, for in Los Angeles the word of Pio Pico counted for a great deal and public pressure was something not even Zeke Wooston would dare to challenge. Her fandango would be popular with the pleasure-loving Californios, and the knowledge that she had money, even if not readily available, would make any move to force her from the ranch decidedly unpopular.

Too many were in the same position. Cash was

always in short supply and many of the wealthiest saw little actual money from one year to the next. Most of the Americans or Europeans who had come to California had married into local families, had become Mexican citizens, and adopted the ways of the community. Wooston had stood aside from all that and was not popular.

Nor was his connection with Micheltorena popular. The governor had made enemies, and his refusal to curb the excesses of the army was making him more enemies. The casual, easy-going Californios could handle their own affairs, and on more than one occasion had banded together to pursue horse thieves or fight off attacks by bands of Indians from the desert.

Sean left his mother talking to a woman on the street and walked to the corner. Despite the Señora's confidence, he was worried.

Zeke Wooston was not a Californio and did not have the tolerant, somewhat casual attitude that was typical of them. Fernandez was a dangerous man, ready to take any advantage, as was Russell. Tomas Alexander? Well, Tomas would be more careful, and if possible, more dangerous.

Sean's eyes searched the street. The pueblo was small, but there were many places where a man might keep out of sight. He glanced at Wooston's office, but there was no sign of movement, no activity. It could be possible they had not yet found their way from the mountains.

He turned on his heel and strolled back the way he had come.

His mother turned to him, and he was again struck by her great beauty. If there was gray in her hair it was not visible, and if there were lines on her face he could not see them. "Come, Sean. We will go back. I wish to stop along the way."

The air was clear, the sky blue. He looked again to the hills where no clouds gathered. The Santa Monicas curved around, and in the distance he could see other mountains lifting their raw backs against the sky.

This was home, this sunny land along the sea with the mountains to shield it from the desert beyond. This was the place where he planned to live out his years, and he wanted no other. Yet he could see the changes that were coming, although many of the Californios still lived in their dreams of a peaceful, quiet world secluded from all that lay outside.

The coming of such men as Stearns, Wilson, Wolf-skill, and the others should have been a warning of what lay ahead. These were hard but honest men, energetic and accustomed to competition and the drive to succeed, and their coming could not help but bring changes. It was these changes for which they must prepare.

In a land where the sun shone nearly every day of the year, where cattle ran the hills in thousands, where anything grew almost without effort, it was too easy to sit back and relax. The trouble was that the men from eastern America and Europe who were now coming had lived in no such easy land and loved the struggle for existence.

His mother had grasped that at once, as soon as she met the first of them. Each day saw them out and doing, and their Californio neighbors smiled at their energy as one smiles at an excited child.

He remembered what the Señora had said, "Remember, Sean. These men are different. They have come and they like it here, and more will come. They will move fast, they will work hard, and in the end they will own it all."

In New England and in northern Europe the seasons were short and the air brisk. One had little time to do what needed to be done. In California the seasons merged, dreamed one into the other, and what was not done today could be done tomorrow.

Sean looked again along the street and eased his Paterson into a better position on his hip. He helped his mother to her saddle and handed her the reins.

Del Campo and Polanco came from a cantina and swung to their saddles. A man came from the cantina behind them, and Del Campo turned his mount to face him. "There was something, Señor? You wished to speak?"

"I speak when I wish. I do not now wish." He was a surly fellow with a knife scar over his right eye and what looked like an old powder burn on his right hand.

Del Campo walked his horse slowly forward. "Do not forget me when you wish to speak," he said gently. "I shall be listening." He smiled, showing white, even teeth.

The scarred man only stared at him, unsmiling. Del Campo wheeled his horse, stirring a cloud of dust, then he galloped after the Señora. Polanco had stayed off to one side, apparently unaware, but the man with the scarred face was not fooled.

Fernandez came from the cantina behind him. "Who are they, Diego? I do not know them."

"Nor I, but they are bad, amigo, ver' bad. I feel it. They are no strangers to the knife, not those."

Fernandez walked back inside, spurs jingling. He walked to a back table where Zeke Wooston sat with Tomas. "It is talked about everywhere," he said. "The Señora has spent gold. She will give a fandango. She has bought much, ordered more, and paid in gold."

Wooston swore. He swore slowly, bitterly, emphatically, giving the words an ugly twist. "Gold! And we were *that* close!"

"The fandango," Fernandez said, "will bring them all to her house. You can do nothing, Señor."

"I'll show them! By the Lord Harry, I'll—!" He broke off suddenly. "Has King-Pin come in?"

"No, Señor. Nor Francisco. I think they look for the gold, Señor."

"Then they'd better come here with it! By God, I didn't hire them to go runnin' off when they're needed."

Fernandez shrugged. "Maybe they cannot come, Señor. Maybe they are dead . . . or gone."

"*Gone?*" Wooston stared at him. "What's that mean?"

"The Old One," Fernandez said. "Follow him into the mountains and sometimes you come back, sometimes not."

"Nonsense!"

Fernandez shrugged. "Perhaps, Señor. It is odd, I think that they never find them . . . not even the bodies . . . they find nothing."

Chapter 15

King-Pin Russell rode into a clearing and drew up, waiting for Francisco. He had become aware that despite his companion's seeming boldness, he was dropping back more and more, and it made Russell uneasy.

He sat very still, listening.

That was it . . . the silence. Why couldn't there be some sound? What was it about these mountains? About this place?

He turned in his saddle, looking all about. There were only mountains, only rocky, brush-covered or pine-clad hills. There were canyons or draws here and there that led to . . . what?

Nothing, probably. Just back to some spot where the water had started a cut into the rock. He wet his lips, considered, and after a bit lifted his canteen and uscrewed the cap for a short drink. He rinsed his mouth carefully, holding it there for a time, then swallowed. His eyes were busy.

The gold must be up here. This was where they had come, and from somewhere up here they had turned back. If he could find the source of that gold . . . to hell with Wooston and the rest of them. He'd take a bit of it, enough of it, and ride right out of here for the north. He could hole up somewhere around Monterey until he could get a ship. Then after awhile he'd come back for more gold. By that time Zeke Wooston would be, hopefully, out of the picture.

Francisco?

He spat. To hell with Francisco. The Mexican would probably try to kill him as soon as they located the gold but he would do it first. Then he'd get out by himself.

He heard the faint footfalls of a horse, and then Francisco appeared, easy in the saddle.

"Where y' been? I figured you was lost."

Francisco shrugged. "I thought my horse had thrown a shoe. It hadn't though. It took me just a little while."

No use arguing. Of course, Francisco was lying. He simply wanted to bring up the rear far enough back so that any trouble that came upon them would strike Russell first. Well, so be it.

"Run out of tracks?" King-Pin asked. "They surely come this way."

Francisco rode past, made a wide sweep, came up with nothing, and began at once to search more carefully.

Still nothing.

Contemptuous at first, he now became irritated. Yet he could find no tracks.

Suddenly a stone fell down among the rocks, bounding from rock to rock. And in that instant, Russell's gun was out and ready. Francisco looked on thoughtfully. Very fast . . . very, very fast.

Only the stone rattling, then quiet. The same quiet as before. Not simply a stillness, but a total absence of sound.

Sweat trickled down the back of Russell's neck. He mopped it with his bandanna, then pointed. "I figure they went along the back side of the mountain."

Francisco looked at the direction with no relish. Dark pine forests alternating with rocky slopes. Not good riding, any of it, and beyond broken crags along a ridge and great tumbled slabs of rock.

"You're the tracker," Russell suggested. "You'd better lead off."

Francisco walked his horse forward, scouting a way through the rocks. They had gone a quarter of a mile before he suddenly said, "Ha!" and pointed.

Russell saw it, after a moment of searching. The cut made by the outer edge of a horse's shoe. It was the trail.

He looked ahead with misgiving, but followed on. If there was gold he meant to have it. He had covered country much like this in many places in the West, so why did this give him that edgy, haunted feeling? Why did he feel that unseen eyes were watching him?

They rode into the pines, a dark, silent place where they wove a slow trail among the pillared trunks. On these trees the growth only started when high off the ground, yet there were other pines here with gray-green, long needles. The trail dipped down, then went up between the rocks and among a thicker stand of pines.

Twice they lost the trail, twice they found it again more by chance than by good sense. On their left ahead of them was a great gouged-out hollow in the ridge. The trail seemed to stop there, and Francisco, casting about, suddenly called him.

King-Pin walked his horse over to him. The ground was marked and scarred by horse tracks. Here the horses had been tied, evidently for some time.

"They walked," Russell said. "It can't be far now."

Francisco looked slowly about him. Gold tinged the ridge beyond Beartrap Creek. The hollow was in shadow now. Darkness came swiftly in these closed-in places where ridges held off the light.

"We'd better camp. We'll find it in the morning."

Russell got down. A thin trickle of water came down from the hollow. He tasted it . . . not bad. "All right," he said.

He was a tough, bitter man with no loyalties, and no ideals. He wanted money for gambling, for women, for power. Yet the few times he had money it had not lasted, and he was left with nothing. He dreamed of the big strike, the big success that would leave him with money for everything. He had not grasped the fact that he was one of those to whom success was a stranger because he lacked persistence. He was forever grasping at chances to get rich in one swift move, and failure taught him nothing.

He sneered at the vaqueros who herded cattle for other men, he had only contempt for hard-working citizens of any kind, never seeming to realize that even the poorest lived better than he did, year in and year out, and without fear of the law.

He had courage and skill with guns. He had belief in his ability to outfight any man and believed himself smarter than most, with no evidence whatever to prove it. He had worked for a number of other men who planned crimes and always for smaller pay than he had expected. In his life there was always a Zeke Wooston who somehow skimmed the cream, but he never asked himself why this was so.

He invariably pictured those who were successful as lucky or thieves who stole what they had by devices imagined but unknown.

Now he was sure he would find the gold. He never doubted the legend of the gold because to doubt it would mean to doubt his whole existence. The gold had to be there, but if somehow he failed to get it he would shift quickly to another treasure to be stolen.

As for Sean Mulkerin, Russell had no doubt he could defeat him in any kind of a fight, although he would prefer it to be with guns. He was wary only of Wooston, for Wooston was more than a danger to be faced. He was a shrewd, conniving man. If Russell respected any man it was Wooston. In California, as in many other lands, death could be bought, and Wooston had money and was friendly with Captain Nick Bell. Russell knew far too much about Bell for comfort. Bell could kill, or have someone killed because he was the law.

Each man carried a little food and they prepared it now. They had eaten and were drinking coffee by the fire when they heard the sound.

At first it seemed far off, then close by. It sounded like someone chanting, but no words could be distinguished.

Francisco crossed himself quickly, and Russell shifted his cup to his left hand and reached for his rifle. He glanced over his shoulder and saw nothing but the darkness beyond the circle of firelight.

The sound vanished, and Russell wet his lips with his tongue. Wind, probably, he told himself, yet it was no wind that he had ever heard before.

"Funny sound," he said, trying to keep his tone casual. "What could it be?"

Francisco shrugged, looking carefully around him. "I do not know, Señor. I think when morning comes it is better we go from here."

"You joking? You mean leave without the gold?"

"Sometimes gold is very expensive, Señor. Perhaps the gold belongs to ghosts. Perhaps only the Old One knows these ghosts."

"I don't believe in ghosts," Russell said, wondering if the statement sounded as hollow as it was. He did not, he told himself, believe in ghosts . . . but what was that sound?

Maybe wind in the rocks . . . but there was no wind. Maybe contraction caused by the chill of evening, but in what? Where?

"Let's get some sleep," he suggested. But he did not feel at all like sleeping.

He gathered wood that lay close about and stacked it near the fire.

"Zeke must be back to Tomas' cantina already," he said, wishing he was there also.

"I think so," Francisco agreed. The Mexican was staying close to the fire, too. Francisco arranged his blankets near the fire, then lay down. He did not, Russell noted, remove his boots.

"I think tomorrow I will go back," Francisco said.

"What's the matter? You scared?"

Francisco looked at him. "Like you, Señor. There is gold that is not for human hands to touch. I am thinking this is such gold."

"The Mulkerins touched it. They took some of it a couple of times."

"The Old One is their friend."

"You'll feel different, come daylight."

"Perhaps, Señor. But I hope I am not such a fool."

133

Resting his head on his arm, he closed his eyes, and Russell was alone with his thoughts. He let his eyes scan the darkness. Anything might be out there . . . but what was he? A scared kid? There ain't such things as ghosts.

He added wood to the fire and rolled up in his blankets, a pistol in his hand. The fire crackled, a low wind moaned in the treetops, somewhere a stone rattled.

He awoke suddenly. He didn't know how long he had been asleep. He lay quiet, listening.

The night was still, but suddenly he caught a faint sound of hoof beats. Faint and far-off, but hoof beats. He sat up quickly and looked around and in an instant he knew what had happened. He had known, instinctively, since he heard those first far-off sounds.

Francisco was gone.

He reached for his gun, started to rise. In a moment of blind rage he wanted only to pursue Francisco and kill him, but he realized his chances of overtaking the Mexican were slight. The man knew this country better that he, and Francisco had a good lead.

Getting up he gathered a few sticks and built up his fire. Dawn was far away.

The coffeepot was still at the edge of the coals so he nudged it closer. He tugged his boots on, stood up, and stamped his feet. He picked up his gun and slid it into the clumsy holster.

His rage subsided and he decided it was the best thing that could have happened. Now he alone would find the gold, and he alone would know where it was. That is, he and the Mulkerin outfit.

He could take care of that in due time, if Zeke Wooston did not.

He would wait until daylight, then hunt for the place where the Mulkerins had gotten their gold. He would load up whatever he could carry and start for the coast.

He could even ride back to Los Angeles, tell Wooston that Francisco had left him and that he'd had a bad time finding his way out of the hills. Let them think he had found nothing.

The night now seemed like any other night. The spooky feeling was gone. He added more wood to the fire, drank more coffee, and saddled his horse. When he returned to the fire a faint light was showing in the east.

An hour later he was riding. The tracks were plain here, tracks coming out of that hollow, that horseshoe-like place in the mountain wall. He rode his horse as far as he could, watered it at the small creek, then tied it on a small patch of grass.

Taking his rifle he started up the creek.

It was an hour before he found the cave. The terrace before it puzzled him. Flat as a floor, free of all large stones, packed very solid as if rolled by something heavy. It looked like some sort of a working area and it puzzled him.

When he saw the cave he was wary. Rifle ready, he approached it. He spoke, and there was no reply. His lips felt dry and he glanced around, seeing nothing. His eyes swept the high rim . . . was someone watching? Was the cave a trap?

He was thinking like a kid again. He stepped into the cave and stopped. On the packed sand of the cave floor lay Juan, the Old One.

He lay perfectly still as if he had merely closed his eyes. Russell touched his hand . . . cool . . . not really cold.

Was he dead? Russell lifted an eyelid. The Indian was dead, all right.

Straightening up, he glanced around. Seeing the pots

he checked them . . . empty. From one he shook a tiny fleck of gold dust.

Damn!

Was that all there was? He started to turn away and suddenly felt a chill go through him.

The body was gone.

Chapter 16

For an instant he stood riveted, a cold prickling traveling along his spine and up the back of his neck. His tongue, gone suddenly dry, fumbled at drier lips. Very slowly, he lowered his hand to his gun.

He was having trouble breathing, as though he had been struck suddenly in the pit of the stomach. His eyes, like those of a trapped animal, moved warily from side to side fearful of what they might see.

The cave was empty. There was nothing there, nothing at all.

He did not move. His muscles seemed stiff, and when he tried to swallow he had to struggle to do it.

Carefully, he drew his gun. The cave mouth was empty, outside there was sunlight. He crouched down, his back against the cave wall. His eyes went again to the place where the Old One's body had lain.

The marks of it were there. That, at least, had not been an illusion. The marks were there, and something else he must not have noticed before. The tracks of sandals . . .

Of woven sandals. His tongue managed to wet his dry lips. He could see the marks of two sets of sandals on either side of the place where the Old One had lain.

Sandals?

That was silly. He was imagining things. Those tracks or whatever they were had to have been there before.

They must have been.

Only they were not.

He straightened up slowly. No use staying here, the gold was gone. It was time to get out. Yet the gold must have come from here, from somewhere around. Gold did not just appear out of thin air. He told himself that, several times.

Circling to avoid the spot where the old man's body had been, he eased out of the cave mouth into the sunlight. All was quiet. The terrace outside was empty. It was very flat, right down to the edge of the creek. Like a floor. Maybe it had been a floor at some time.

He mopped his face with a handkerchief and squinted his eyes against the morning sun. Heat waves shimmered beyond the terrace. He'd never seen them so close before. Heat waves usually only showed themselves at some distance.

He mopped his face again and looked slowly around. No signs of mining, no arrastra, no rusted picks or shovels, no evidence of placer mining.

Where the devil had that body gone to?

He must go. He wanted to get away from here, far, far away, yet there was a deep-seated fear within him . . . would they let him go?

And who were *they?*

He still held the pistol in his hand. He walked slowly, putting each foot down carefully, walking as if in a trance, back to the trail. Only he could not seem to see the trail. It was here . . . right here.

Brush, bare sand, some scattered rock, but no trail. Surely he had come in from the east? Of course, he could see the great gap in the mountain over there. He stumbled into the brush. Just head for that gap and he'd find his way out.

What could have happened to that trail? Of course, it was probably just behind some brush, he'd just cut too short or something. He would come upon it any time now. Anyway, there was the gap. Head for that and he'd be out where his horse was.

It was very hot in the brush where no breeze could reach him. He started to hurry, sweat streaked his face, ran down his body under his shirt. He stumbled, almost went to his knees and straightened up. There was a bush right before him. He must have turned halfway around when he almost fell. He changed direction, pushed his way between clinging bushes and thrust on.

Suddenly he came up short. He had faced around and was heading back. He mopped his face, stared wildly around and plunged on again. When he fought himself free of the brush his shirt was torn. He had been carrying his pistol in his hand and now he thrust it back in the holster.

He stood in a small open space among clumps of brush and trees, panting for breath. God, but it was *hot!* He stared around him. Where the devil was that trail?

Due to the height of the brush he could no longer see the gap and only a portion of the rim. He started on, then paused.

On the sand, right before him, were the distinct tracks of sandals.

Two feet, side by side.

Only they stood where no man could have stood due to the bulge of the brush. They were there, as if someone had stood there only a moment before, looking at him.

He turned away, found a space between trees and walked through. Ahead of him there was a flat rock

138

about waist high, standing between two trees. A third tree was behind it, and the rock looked almost like a stone picnic table.

Or a butcher's block. Or an altar. Or both.

He had started forward to sit down on it, wanting a rest. Now he backed away, until the brush brought him up short. An altar?

What kind of a silly thought was that? An altar in such a place as this? Of course, he supposed, the Indians might have used altars. He had little idea of how they worshiped or even if they did.

Speaking of Indians . . . what happened to that body?

And those sandal tracks?

Still, the place where a rock had been lying might look something like a sandal track, or a lot of things might have caused it. Anyway there were no Indians around here. Francisco said that.

But Francisco was gone. He had fled in the night. Why?

King-Pin Russell looked again at the altar. Then for the first time he realized that three tracks came out of the woods leading up to the altar.

Like the tracks of a gigantic turkey three trails emerged from the brush and ended at the altar, if altar it was.

He mopped the sweat from his face and neck. Which way to go? Damn it, how could he have lost that trail? If he could only see over the brush, locate the gap. After all, it *was* the only way out. If he could locate the gap he had only to go down the slope to it.

He looked around for a tree to climb, but there were none near that would bear his weight. The highest place and the best footing were on the altar.

He started toward it, then stopped, a curious reluctance coming over him. *What kind of a damn' fool you gettin' to be?* he asked himself. *You're like a kid or some silly woman.*

He rested his hands on the altar, then vaulted easily to the top. Standing on tiptoes he peered over the brush and saw the gap . . . just over there.

His vision blurred. He shook his head, feeling slightly dizzy and nauseous. What was the matter, anyway? Heat waves shimmered and the horizon became vague, unreal. What was the matter? What was happening to him? He swayed, clutched at the empty air, and fell. He seemed to fall for a long, long time, then smashed against the ground.

The earth seemed to tip and roll and he clutched at it, his brain spinning in slow, dipping rolls. He tried to rise but his muscles had no strength, he tried to think, but his thoughts would not focus.

He lifted his head and the heat waves shimmered and the trees showed through them, but there was no solidity anywhere, not in the trees, nor yet in the mountains. He was neither wholly conscious nor unconscious and yet vaguely he seemed to see the shimmering air, seemed to hear the shuffling sounds of sandals, seemed to see the unreal shapes of Indians in the dancing heat waves.

Were they near or far? Were they real or only figments of his distraught mind?

The Indians, like no Indians he had ever seen, came slowly from the heat waves.

"He pursued the Old One," one said.

"He was the enemy of the Señora," another said.

"He is evil," said a third.

"If he goes now he will tell others of this place," the first one said.

"So he must not go," said the second, "not for a long, long time."

Was it only in his mind? Was he vaguely conscious, or was this a dream, a nightmare, a haunting unreality come to torture his delirium?

He felt hands grasp his arms and legs. He tried to move, and he could not. He felt himself lifted . . . carried. . . .

Hilo came up from the schooner to help, and several of the Chumash, who had helped before, came to the ranch. They dug holes and sank posts, slender posts to hold up roofs made of tules for shade. The oak trees near the house offered shade also, and a space was roped off for the dancing.

Sean rode out on the hill near Las Flores Canyon and shot three steers to be butchered on the spot. One was brought in upon a cart after the meat was dressed and hung up in the shade. Two were to be roasted upon spits.

A dozen women had appeared, some from the homes of vaqueros, some from the pueblo, and they bustled about busy with a thousand things, cooking, decorating, cleaning, preparing for the fiesta. After killing the meat and seeing that it arrived safely, Sean kept out of the way.

At one side he spoke to Polanco. "It is a time to be careful," he said, "we want no trouble, but if it comes —?"

"We will be ready, Señor. It is understood."

Tennison came up from the *Lady Luck*. "Down to Pedro," he said, "there's talk around. King-Pin's disappeared."

"Disappeared?"

"He never came back from the mountains. Wooston is hinting he was killed, murdered."

"He probably just got lost. He would not be the first."

"No, he wouldn't. But that ain't what Wooston has in mind. Wooston hasn't said yet, so far's I could make out, but he sort of implies maybe it was you who did him in."

"Well, I didn't."

"Just figured you should know." Tennison watched the women passing to and fro, then said, "Cap'n, what does happen back in yonder?"

Sean shrugged. "Look . . . it is mountain and semi-desert. There's water if a man knows where to look, and if he doesn't he can kill himself looking. If a man gets lost the best thing he can do is head west. Sooner or later he will come to the sea, if he lasts long enough."

"What about all this talk of ha'nts and such-like?"

"Who knows?" Sean thought of the mountain valleys and canyons, so still, so alone, and yet—

"Every country has its secrets, and every people their superstitions. Who is to say what is and what is not true? One of the stories current among the Indians is that they came out of a cave or a hole in the ground into this world. That may be pure symbolism. It may imply they were simply born of the earth, but it might mean just what it says.

"The more you wander around back there the more you're willing to believe anything the Indians believe. Walk up any one of those canyons alone and see how you feel. You won't go a hundred yards before you wonder if something is not watching.

"You don't get it in the open desert as much, but wherever there are canyons, rocks, peaks and such, you get that feeling. Now maybe it is just a feeling . . . but maybe something is watching.

"Once when the Old One talked to me he told me they knew about me, and they knew about the Señora, and they were friendly to us, but he did not tell me who 'they' were."

"Knew a sailorman one time, he was a great talker, but he'd been 'most everywhere. He allowed how there was other worlds right next to this one . . . something about time and space . . . I couldn't make out just what he meant. He said he was a disciple of Pythagoras, whatever that meant, but he argued that a man could pass right from one world into the next, and maybe come back, too. Only the time was different . . . or could be different."

"I've heard such talk. You get out in those hills alone and soon you are ready to believe almost anything."

He paused, listening to the pat-pat-i-pat-pat of women's hands slapping tortillas. "Out east people talk of all manner of mysterious things. That's India, China, and places like that, but they don't know this country. The old people here . . . I'm not sure if they were what we called Indians or not . . . they had their own mysteries.

"You look at one of these Indians. Maybe he's just a man who hunts wild game, plants a few crops, herds sheep or loafs around the village . . . but maybe he's relative to something that's old . . . older than any of our history, older than there's any figure for.

"They say one time this land north of here was covered with ice . . . a glacier. But what was there before the ice came? What would be left of an adobe house if a thousand feet of ice lay over it? Grinding down, pushing, pulverizing. But there are some things that cannot be lost as long as one man or woman exists, and that's the memories of older times.

"If the children don't listen, of course, and if they don't want to hear, then something is lost, but somewhere it lingers on. Somewhere there's been a record left . . . if a man could find it . . . or if he was really sure he wanted to."

"Of course he'd want to. If he had any brains he'd want to."

Sean smiled wryly. "Maybe . . . and maybe not. As long as a man gets up in the morning, pulls on his pants, stomps into his boots, and goes about his business the world is a simple, comfortable, understandable place. You get to delving . . . delving deep . . . well, there's no telling what you'll bring up.

"One time off Cape Comorin at the southern tip of India we were becalmed for a few hours. We'd been coasting down from Ceylon, figuring to round the cape and go up the coast to catch the trades across to Africa. Becalmed there, we tried dragging a net for fish. We got fish, all right, but we got some other stuff, too. We got some pieces of broken pottery . . . such pictures you never saw . . . and the hand and arm of a statue. It was carved from stone, beautiful thing, only the hand had six fingers."

"That's funny," Ten commented, "there's a cave drawing back yonder above Malibu with a hand with six fingers."

Sean got up. "We'd better go lend a hand," he said quietly. And then he added, "I've seen such tracings of hands . . . several had six fingers."

"What's it mean?"

Sean shrugged. "Must've been a people one time who ran to six fingers . . . and they got around. One way or another."

Chapter 17

On the day of the fiesta the first of the guests arrived shortly after dawn. A group of six riding horseback from up the coast, they had camped on the shore the previous night and brought a fine catch of fish to contribute to the food supply.

There were three women, one of them young and very bright-eyed and excited at the thought of the fandango. There was one man, an almost grown boy, and a small girl.

From then on they came in a steady stream, a stream that never ceased until all the ranchos within miles were represented.

The Señora was everywhere, superintending the preparation of food, the decorations, the shades, everything.

Polanco came to Sean shortly before noon. "Señor? There are men in the hills who do not come down. I have seen them."

"What are they doing?"

"They watch, Señor. There is one who goes and comes back. He goes further back, toward the ridge. I think he meets with someone there."

"Thanks. Keep an eye on them, Polanco, and be ready."

The white teeth flashed. "I am always ready, Señor. It is that one wishes to live, no?"

Sean was standing in the shade when three men started across the yard toward him. They were lean men, and tall, with Mexican spurs and battered, flat-brimmed hats. One wore a buckskin vest, fringed in Indian fashion.

"Howdy, Sean," the speaker was a man with a narrow, raw-boned face and gray eyes that smiled easily. "Ain't seen you for a spell."

"Johnny Mims! I'll be damned! You back at El Monte?"

"Uh-huh. We run into some horse thieves out yonder. Had some shootin', but we come on in anyway."

He gestured to the men with him. "Reckon you remember Bill Honeycutt? Well, this here's Larkin Campbell. He joined up with us down on the Rio Grande last trip." He glanced around. "Hear you been havin' trouble."

"Money trouble, mostly," Sean replied, "but Zeke Wooston is behind it. He wants this place."

"You have trouble and you don't let us share it, you're less of a friend than I think," Mims said quietly. "We've got no use for Wooston. In fact, those hoss thieves may have had a mite of help from around the pueblo. Maybe somebody promised to buy any stock they come up with."

"Do you know that?"

"Well, I got no evidence that will stand in a court of law, but then we ain't just figurin' on takin' it to no court. Out yonder in the desert it's a fur piece to the law so we just have to make do."

"Enjoy yourselves, boys," Sean suggested. "There's plenty to eat and drink, and the crowd's a-gathering."

"We come along a pretty good gait," Honeycutt said, "but we passed nearly fifty outfits between here an' Rancho La Brea."

Suddenly Larkin Campbell spoke. "This here Ortega outfit? Will they be comin' to this shindig?"

"They probably will. Nobody misses a fiesta unless he's sick or out of the country. Do you know them?"

"Only by name. I hear they make the finest riatas in the country, and I need me a new rope."

"They do that," Sean agreed. "I like the four-strand

for rough work, although they weave an eight-strand that's beautiful to see. But they'll be around, you can be sure of that."

Sean crossed to his mother who was arranging some flowers on a table under the tule-covered shade. "The boys from El Monte are here."

She looked up, flashing him a quick smile. "Keep them quiet, Sean. You know how they are."

He chuckled. "They just like a good time. All those Texans like to kick up their heels just to hear their spurs jingle." Then he added, "They've no love for Wooston."

"Good! We can use friends."

All morning they came. Lugos, Avilas, Sepulvedas, and families who had been traveling for several days, stopping at intervening ranchos, coming along slowly on horseback or in the cumbersome carretas drawn by oxen.

They were gaily dressed, their horses as beautifully caparisoned as themselves. By the time noon had come, two dozen carretas stood on the outskirts, and dozens of saddled horses at the hitching rails. Others had been turned into the pole corrals. Here and there someone was singing with a guitar, but the preparations continued, with much bustling to and fro by the women, many excited cries, and much laughter.

Sean went inside to comb his hair before the small mirror in his mother's room, the only one in the house. Yet he had come there in part for a moment alone.

Zeke Wooston would not doubt their possession of gold, of that he was sure. Wooston would not doubt it because it was his belief in that gold that made him want the ranch. The smuggling, of course, was another reason he wanted the ranch.

From the coast at Paradise Cove or any one of the several coves along the coast there was easy access to the interior by way of the canyons. From there goods could be brought into Los Angeles, and the demand was great. Moreover, most of the people in California did not look upon smuggling as a crime, for the laws against trade with foreigners were strict and goods hard to obtain from Mexico, and very expensive.

Wooston would believe in the gold, but the fact that he would now expect them to pay the money owed would in no way stop him from seeking to acquire the ranch. Now that gold had once more been found would only whet his appetite, and Wooston was not one to hesitate over something he wanted.

He could use influence with Micheltorena, but there was little the governor could do . . . unless the Señora, Brother Michael, and he were dead.

There would be no heirs, the ranch would be seized by the governor, and then they might gain possession.

Yet Sean doubted if that was the means they would use. They would not want to trust even the governor, who might easily give the land to someone else or keep it in his own possession. Certainly, they would try to find some other way.

He hitched his belt into a better set on his hips and scowled at the mirror.

How?

And where was King-Pin Russell?

His thoughts returned to the matter of payment. They could now borrow the money, he believed, for everyone believed they had access to gold. Yet even if they could not borrow it they would have gained time, and time was what was needed.

Yet he, who alone could handle the *Lady Luck*, dared not leave on a trading voyage. They could, he believed, get together something of a cargo, partly from their own ranch, partly from others. There would be a profit if he went somewhere besides Mexico.

Sitka? The Russians to the north needed wheat, and they had furs to trade. Furs were in demand in China and on the East Coast.

He checked the Paterson Colt. It was fully loaded and ready. He ran his fingers down his knife scabbard and glanced out through the open door.

More people were arriving. Polanco had said some men were lurking in the hills. Who, and why? Men of Wooston's, without a doubt, but they might be men come to take Mariana away, and against them he would have little defense. After all, she had been betrothed to Andres. Her uncle had arranged it. For most of these people that would be sufficient, and he would be in the wrong. At the same time the romance of her flight to his ship would be intriguing.

He walked outside and watched the people circulating. Musicians were tuning their instruments, trying a few bars of this song or that, and soon the dancing would start.

He watched the crowd. It was a shifting, colorful scene, and one he loved. He was more of a spectator than a participant at these things, but he loved them nonetheless, yet there was an uneasiness upon him.

It was the feeling he had sometimes before a bad storm at sea, when you could feel the weather making up. Yet this was no storm of that kind, this was something else entirely.

Trouble was coming, and he did not know how or where. Wooston . . . Andres . . . it could be either.

Or it could be King-Pin.

Montero strolled over to him. "It is a good night for the dance," he said quietly, "but I do not think it a good one for us."

"You feel it, too?"

Montero said nothing for a moment, then: "I do. It is in the wind . . . or it is because we know it must

149

come. I do not know what it is, but there will be trouble."

"I am glad Mims is here."

Montero chuckled softly. "He is a wild one, but a good man. I do not think he will be an old man. Not that one. But neither will a lot of others."

"The Old One is gone."

"Yes . . . he will be missed, I think. He was a good man."

"What did you know about him, Jesus?"

Montero shrugged. "No more than you, I think. He spoke once of a door one could pass through, that there were times to go and times to come, and that there were other worlds beyond."

He paused a moment. "The gold may have come through such a door. It may have been an offering."

Sean Mulkerin's forefathers had talked of leprechauns and banshees, and knew of the old Celtic gods. Ireland is an old land where ghosts linger, and shadows of ancient memories are in the rocks and the fens. He had no superstitions as such, yet he did not doubt there were things of which he knew nothing, and perhaps veils beyond which he could not see.

"I do not know," he said, "for whom such an offering would be made."

"Who knows, Señor? Often the offerings to gods are made even when the names of the gods are forgotten. Habit is forever with us, I think, and the old beliefs may wither but they do not die."

They walked outside together and stood under the porch. Sean's eyes went to the hills, brush-covered and silent in the sun. What eyes watched from there? They seemed so innocent, yet he had found lonely places out there, ghostly in their silence.

The dancing had begun. El Tecolero, the master of the dance, had begun it with a *la jota,* a simple but lovely dance. He watched, but his thoughts were not with them. There would be trouble, he knew it. He turned to speak to Montero, but the Californio was gone.

Polanco was across the yard near the pole corral where the horses were. Johnny Mims was dancing, but Larkin Campbell and Bill Honeycutt were standing at one side, smoking and watching.

Suddenly there was a rush of horses' hoofs up the trail and several men, six or seven at least, rode up. Andres, on a splendid black horse, was in the lead. He rode magnificently. Tomas Alexander was there, and Fernandez. The others were a hard-bitten lot.

Sean saw Honeycutt move a bit to one side to have a better view.

Sean walked across the small dancing area, moving through the dancers. When he emerged from the crowd he was facing Andres.

"It is a fandango," he said quietly, "we dance here, and we sing. If you come for the dancing and singing you are welcome, and so are your friends."

"And if I do not?" Andres' eyes were cool but taunting.

"Then you are not welcome, and as a caballero you would go away until the fiesta is finished."

"You teach *me?*"

"I remind you."

Andres laughed, but there was no humor in it. "All right, there shall be only the fiesta." His white teeth flashed. "After that I shall kill you."

Sean Mulkerin smiled deprecatingly. "Of course, you will try." He paused. "It is a pity when there are so many girls who like you to die for one who doesn't."

Andres had started to turn, now he wheeled his horse. "It is not I who will die!"

Sean smiled in great good humor. "They always feel

that way until they taste the blade. *Buenos tardes, Señor!*" He turned away.

From the coast road came the creaking and groaning of carretas arriving with more guests, many of them decorated with ribbons of various colors, nearly all filled with girls or young men as well as the older people. Alongside each carreta there were usually several outriders wearing velvet suits with wide-bottomed, slashed pants, or beautifully tanned suits of white buckskin. Sombreros were the order of the day for the men.

Many of the women were elaborately gowned, but some, if their trip had been a long one, brought clothes into which to change. The dancing had begun so many of the newcomers leaped from the carreta or the saddle into the middle of the dance.

Sean moved from group to group, smiling, shaking hands, welcoming his guests. Andres, he noted, seemed to have dropped his anger at the gate and now mixed freely. Yet several of those who had come with him, notably Fernandez, hung upon the fringe of the crowd, glowering.

Honeycutt had moved from near the corral to a position not far from Fernandez. He was a good hand with a guitar, but even during the moments when he played and sang, his eyes were never far from Fernandez.

The others who had come from far-flung haciendas seemed unaware of the trouble. They were laughing, gay, friendly. Sean, who had helped the Lugos round up cattle and wild horses, who knew all those from the surrounding ranches, enjoyed meeting his friends.

Andres, he decided, would probably live up to his agreement to create no trouble as long as the fiesta lasted, but he had made no promises beyond that. Wooston had made no promises at all, and Wooston was not present.

So where was he?

From dance to dance they moved, and Mariana was in the thick of it all.

Suddenly Andres was beside her, and in a moment they were dancing together. And they danced well. Watching them, Sean felt a flash of irritability. Why did he have to come here? Did she love him after all?

They were dancing *la Bamba*, and very well, too, a glass of water upon her head as she moved, spilling not one drop.

Andres, he could see, was good. Better than anybody he had seen, and there were fine dancers among the Lugos, Yorbas, and Estudillos. The young Mexican was quick, lithe, and unbelievably expert.

Sean turned sharply away and went inside. His mother laughed at him. "Jealous? You must not be. It is only the dance."

"But with *him!*"

"Why not with him? He is a very good dancer. Anyway, if it is Andres she loved, then why not find out now? But I think it is only the dance, and she is angry with him, she wants to show him a little, I think, what he is missing."

Suddenly Montero was in the room. "Señor? Señora? There is a man . . . he is by the corral. He would speak with you!"

Chapter 18

Sean Mulkerin turned sharply to follow, then hesitated. He glanced at Montero. "He is alone?"

Montero's face was stiff, his eyes wide. "He has one man with him, Señor. One only."

A sound of hoofs from the trail turned him again.

Dust arose, and through the dust a half-dozen men. Zeke Wooston, Captain Nick Bell, and several soldiers.

Johnny Mims was beside him, from out of nowhere. "You got friends, Sean boy. Stand your ground."

"I do not want shooting here," Sean said quietly. "We will have none."

"May not be that easy," Mims said quietly. "I think they've come for your scalp."

Nick Bell was no respecter of persons. He pushed his horse right across the crowded dance area, followed by his riders. They were a nondescript lot. Wooston looked pleased, too pleased.

"Ah? Sean Mulkerin, is it?" Bell smiled. He was a hard man, utterly vicious, and completely sure of himself as an officer of the province. "You are arrested. We have come to take you to jail."

"And for what?"

"The murder of King-Pin Russell," Wooston replied. "You will be taken to jail."

"You have found him?"

Bell shrugged. "It does not matter, Señor Mulkerin. You were his enemy. He disappeared in the mountains where you were. We have men that will swear—"

"I have no doubt of it," Sean replied, "but do you have someone who will swear he is my enemy?"

"It was known! He was riding in pursuit of you!"

"In pursuit? Why was he pursuing me? And why should he be my enemy? If he rode into the mountains it was his own idea."

"He was following you, and he has not come back. You killed him." Nick Bell leaned both hands on the pommel and smiled, a thoroughly unpleasant smile. "So you are to be taken to prison," he smiled again, "where you will be questioned."

Bell was obviously enjoying himself. He had never liked Sean Mulkerin nor his mother, for they had

154

shown nothing but contempt for him. Now it was his turn.

Johnny Mims strolled a little closer. "You don't need to go nowhere you don't want to, Mulkerin," he said quietly. "We got as many men as he has, and better ones."

Bell's smile vanished. There was no fear in Bell and they all knew it. Thug he might be, but he had nerve. "You would go against the law? I can bring more men and more. I can throw you all into prison."

Don Abel Stearns was standing nearby, so were two of the Lugos. His eye caught the movement as they drew closer. They were people of influence and judgment, and he did not like their presence here but there was nothing he could do.

"Señor?" It was Montero again. "I think you must see this man. The one by the corral." He looked around him. "I think you must all see him."

"Bring him here, then."

"It can wait," Bell said abruptly. "Do your business later."

"It cannot wait," Montero said.

Nick Bell's lips tightened with anger. "You talk to me, you cholo? I'll show—"

"Stand where you are!" Eileen Mulkerin's rifle was on his chest, and the crowd gave way to give her a clear field of fire from her position on the porch. "Jesus Montero works for me. You lay a hand on him and I'll kill you."

Bell stopped, staring at her. "Put that gun down!" he snapped.

"Couple of 'em over here, too," Bill Honeycutt said mildly. "Be quite a contest to see who gets lead into you first, and how much. I figure I can, but Lark here, he always did figure he could shoot faster than me, so maybe it would be him. As for the Señora there, I don't know whether you ever seen her shoot or not. I seen her drop a runnin' antelope seventy yards off with a quick shot. You're closer an' a bigger target."

Bell sat very still. He knew all about those Texans from El Monte. There were quite a few of them, a wild, roistering, hell-for-leather lot who respected courage and little else. They were hard workers, but troublemakers. And he had no doubt at all about their shooting.

Several years before a small colony of them had moved in and settled there, and since then they had run cattle, a few had become farmers, and a few were in business. They were good people to leave alone.

He was wary now. "All right," he said crisply, "see to your business."

"Bring the man here," Sean repeated, and Montero turned and walked away.

For a few minutes they stood in uneasy silence. The music and the dancing had stopped. A few of the visitors had seated themselves and were drinking at the tables under the awning.

Montero came back around the corner of the house and he was walking beside an Indian who led a burro. Upon the burro's back there was a man . . . an old, old man.

They stared. Zeke Wooston suddenly dismounted and walked to the burro. He caught the old man by the arm, staring into his face. Then he dropped the arm as if burned and stepped sharply back.

"Russell!" he said, almost choking on the name. "By God, it's King-Pin!"

They crowded around, helping the old man from the saddle. His clothing was ragged and old, and the man who wore them was only a shadow of the powerful King-Pin.

He leaned against the burro, jaws agape, drooling a little, his eyes vacant and empty. "Zeke," he muttered, "Zeke, I—"

His voice trailed off and he stopped.

They drew back from him, backing slowly away. Wooston's pallor was that of a man who has seen a ghost.

"That's not Russell!" Bell said sharply. "Russell was a young man. He couldn't have been more than thirty! This man . . . why he must be seventy or eighty years old!"

"That's him," somebody said. "Look at the notches on the gun! Not more'n three weeks ago he was showin' me them notches an' that pistol. Ain't many of them around, anyway."

Carlotta, the housekeeper, came from the house with a glass of wine. She handed it to the old man and he took it in fingers that trembled.

"King-Pin," Honeycutt said, "what happened to you?"

"Lost . . . lost," Russell muttered. "I was lost. Trail disap . . . peared. There was an altar . . . I climbed on it to see . . . fell. Fell for a long time. Injuns got me . . . they taken me."

"Where did they take you?"

He raised his head and looked slowly around, his eyes staring and empty. "I don't know. I just don't know."

"Those Injuns," somebody said, "they didn't take your gun?"

"Paid it no mind," Russell said.

Bell's horse stepped forward. "Are you Russell?" he asked.

"Walter Pendleton Russell. They call me King-Pin. I come from Lancashire to Carolina. I handled a freight team on the Santa Fe Trail. I come west. I—" his voice trailed off and he drank the wine, then dropped the glass, staring as it lay in the dust.

"What about those Injuns?" Somebody asked from the crowd. "Was they Mohaves' Paiutes?"

"Injuns . . . never seen the like . . . carried me off, dropped me . . . just lef' me."

Tomas Alexander edged closer. "The Old One? Did you see him?"

"Dead . . . dead on the sand." The old man was silent for a few moments and then he said, "Cave . . . he was lyin' there. I was huntin' gold . . . turned around . . . he was gone."

"Got up an' walked out," Wooston said.

"Dead," Russell muttered. "That was years . . . years back. I recall—"

"King," Wooston interrupted. "It was only a few days ago! Just up in the mountains!"

The old man stared at him with weak, watery eyes. "Years . . . years back. I seen—" his voice trailed off.

"Better let him sit down," Sean suggested quietly. "The man is old, he is very tired. Lord knows what he's been through."

Eileen Mulkerin lowered her rifle. "Carlotta, take him inside. Give him some wine. Maybe he will eat something."

The Californios had withdrawn and were gathered in groups, talking. The music started again, and the dancing, but there was no heart in it.

"That was King-Pin Russell," Sean said quietly, to Nick Bell. "He's alive, as you can see. You still want to take me in."

Bell shrugged. "He's alive . . . if that's him." He looked curiously at Sean Mulkerin. "You were up there. What happened, anyway?"

"Who knows? Looks like he's aged fifty years."

"That isn't reasonable."

"No, Captain, it isn't."

Bell stared at him. "Mulkerin, you don't believe all that damned nonsense, do you? I mean, all that talk about what happens in the mountains?"

Sean shrugged. "Captain, what happens to one man in the mountains need never happen to another. The Indians lived here long before we came. Do you think it wise to dismiss all they know as superstition? I do not.

"We live in a world, Captain, that none of us know too well, and none of us know it all. I can only say this. My mother went up there with the Old One. The Old One went to sleep on the floor of a cave, and when she called to him to leave, he was dead."

"And Russell found him there?"

"It sounds like it."

"He says the old man was carried off while his back was turned?"

"You heard him, so did I. Captain, there are places up there where the heat waves seem close up, everything is kind of indistinct and unreal. You can't judge distance properly, nor time either."

"What do you suppose happened to him?" Bell mused.

Sean shrugged again. "He says he fell. Maybe shock can do that to a man. Maybe he was carried off, taken somewhere we don't even know about for . . . he says it was for years."

"And we know it was only a few days."

"Do we? A few days to us, maybe years to him. I am not going to try to explain it. I only know the Old One warned my mother about wandering around. When she left, the trail was plain, but when Russell looked for it he could not find it."

"It doesn't make sense," Bell said irritably. He turned his horse and rode away, followed by his troopers.

Zeke Wooston was at the door of the house, talking to the Señora. "But he's one of my men!" he protested. "I'll take what care of him he needs."

"Let him have him, Señora," Sean suggested. "We have no right to hold him."

"But he's an old man! He needs care!"

"Let them care for him," Sean replied. "I do not think he will be around for long."

"What do you mean by that?" Wooston protested.

"Look at him," Sean replied. "Have you really looked at him?"

They turned. Russell sat at the table, his head hanging, his hands lax upon his knees. He seemed to have shrunken visibly. His face was seamed and old. Sean spoke, and after a moment the old man's head lifted, but his eyes were unseeing and after a minute, they dropped.

Wooston stared at the old man, then thought rapidly. Russell had found where the gold came from. He had actually seen the Old One, and if the old man had died there, it must have been the farthest they had gone. Surely, dying, he could have shown them no further along a trail.

Russell, then, knew where the gold came from. Dying or not, he knew. And he could tell Wooston. The big man touched his lips with his tongue, then he smiled. "He was my friend. I will not leave him alone and helpless now. If you will lend us a carreta?"

"Of course," Sean said. "He will need care."

Wooston hurried out, and for a moment Sean, the Señora and Russell were alone.

"Russell?"

The old man looked up, if old man he could be called.

"I was never your enemy. This . . . whatever happened . . . I am sorry."

"I fell," Russell muttered, talking as if to himself. "It was the altar . . . I should not have touched it. I . . . I felt it . . . I felt I should not, but . . . but I had to *see*!"

"It is all right, Mr. Russell," Eileen said quietly. "We hold no grudge against you. You have suffered enough."

His body shook. "I was lost . . . lost! I could not find . . . there was no *way*! Shimmering, Shimmering, shimmering! I got *through* . . . into something, somewhere. I tried to find my way back. I was lost . . . lost.

"Everywhere there were bushes, bushes that clawed and tore at me, I fell again, and I do not know for how long I lay, I got up and suddenly I was *back*. I was on the hills above the sea, and the air was fresh and cool. I was back. I do not know how but I was back."

"He has lost his wits," Wooston had come back into the room. "His mind is wandering."

"Whatever happened to him," Eileen Mulkerin said, "should not happen to any man."

Wooston helped Russell to his feet and they started outside. Sean watched them go, then said to his mother, "I've got to go back, you know. I've got to be sure the Old One was buried."

"Russell said his body vanished."

"Perhaps . . .he might have been delirious even then. His mind does seem to wander. It is not coherent."

"You do not believe that, Sean.'

"No, I don't," he replied honestly. "We'll never know what happened to him. Some terrible shock, or maybe some injury did this to him . . . or some experience. I've heard of men's hair turning white in a single night."

The musicians were playing again, and the mood of depression brought on by Russell's unexpected return and the coming of Nick Bell had vanished. Suddenly it was a fiesta again.

Sean looked quickly around, caught the flashing black eyes of Mariana and moved through the crowd toward her. She looked up laughing, and together they moved off to the dancing.

"It is over then?" she asked, during a pause.

"No," he said quietly, "it is not over. Wooston has gone away, but when the crowd is gone, he will come back, and he still has men hidden up in the hills."

"There will be trouble?"

Sean shrugged. "Who knows? I think there will be. There will be trouble with Zeke Wooston and there will be trouble with Machado . . . he is not finished."

"I danced with him."

"I saw."

"He came and it was a challenge."

"So? Do you want to go back with him? You can, you know."

"With him? *No!*" Her eyes flashed at him. "I will stay . . . with you."

"And my mother," he said, smiling.

"I like her . . . your mother. She is a *woman*."

"Nobody could argue that point. Sometimes I wish—"

"That she would marry again?"

"How did you guess?" He paused. "Yes, I think so, but it would take a strong man, a very strong man, sure of himself . . . and calm. She has fire enough for two."

"And you, Señor?" Her eyes were impudent, challenging. "Will you marry?"

"Someday," he grinned, "someday when I can find a woman who will walk beside me . . . not behind me."

"I think she is not hard to find, this woman. I think you will find her.'

Polanco was suddenly beside him. "Señor? There are men upon the hills . . . more men. They have camped, and they wait."

"So?"

"Señor Wooston is among them . . . and Machado."

He glanced at her. "You see? It is never over. I think someone must die first."

Johnny Mims had been listening to Polanco. "You know somethin', Sean? I'm powerful tired. Boney weary, I am. I think I'll just sort of settle down an' rest up . . . me an' the boys."

Sean glanced toward the hills. There was a reflection of fire at one point among the dark and lonely hills. A breeze from the sea stirred the leaves of the chaparral.

"Polanco," he suggested, "ride down to the *Lady Luck* and tell Tennison to send me two good men, will you? Send them before daylight. I think we'll have visitors."

Chapter 19

Nobody needed to tell Ruiz Beltran how to do the job to which he had been assigned. Nor did Velasco need any instruction.

Beltran had been a hunter of jaguars and wolves for stockmen south of the border. When the government of his state offered a bounty for the scalps of Apaches he had done well, and who was to say whether the scalps on which he collected bounty were not all those of Apaches?

Velasco had been a bandit, a farmer, a vaquero, and, briefly, a soldier.

To kill such a man as Sean Mulkerin was easy. He rode often into the mountains, occasionally to town. The mountains would be better, for many a man went to the mountains who did not return.

As for the Señora, she had hair like a flame. It was easy to see, and there was no chance of a mistake. Nobody else had such hair . . . he had never seen such hair. Nor such a woman.

They had found a seep on a small, out-of-the-way mesa near Saddle Peak, and there they camped among some boulders. The seep was a mere trickle, and apparently known to none but the few birds, and small animals for whom the water was sufficient. Enlarging the basin somewhat they soon had enough water for what was needed. Secure from discovery, they could hide themselves and their horses while studying the land around them. From not far off there was a good position to observe the comings and goings of the ranch.

On the day following their arrival, the fiesta ended with a stream of carretas and riders leaving. All did not depart at once, so they waited. They ate, slept, drank a little wine, and waited.

"One thing at a time, you see?" Beltran suggested. "One day he will ride out alone, and when he does, the time will come."

"And when they come for his body?" Velasco suggested.

"Perhaps. I think maybe when first they take his body to the ranch. She will come out. She with the red hair. How can one make a mistake? But we will shoot . . . both of us."

"And then?"

"We will arrange a meeting with Señor Wooston. We will tell him to bring the money."

"And if he does not?"

"We will kill him. I think maybe we will kill him anyway, when he brings the money. I do not like Señor Wooston too much . . . and he will have more money. Besides, nobody will know what we did if he is killed, also. You see?"

The idea appealed to Velasco. He did not like Wooston, either, and the idea of killing him was appealing. How could you trust such a man?

In Topanga Canyon there was a cantina, a very small place run by a very big woman. Tia Angelena was taller than most men and weighed, it was guessed, some two hundred and fifty pounds, only a few of them fat, and she administered her place of business with a firm and muscular hand. Yet she cared not in the least who they might be or where they came from.

Tia Angelena was a woman of no scruples to speak of but considerable loyalty, and one of these loyalties was to Eileen Mulkerin.

Angelena had upon one occasion some years before been taken ill, and believing it to be cholera, which had appeared briefly in the area, both customers and her few neighbors fled. In that extremity Eileen Mulkerin came riding by, saw no smoke from the chimney and the door standing open. Sensing distress, the Señora dismounted and went in to find Angelena in a coma, the place a mess, the animals starving.

Being a woman of anger and determination, Eileen Mulkerin took charge. Within a matter of minutes she had straightened the bed, the room, and was preparing treatment for Tia Angelena, who did not have cholera but was, nonetheless, very ill.

For three days she stayed and administered to the sick woman until finally she was able to get up and care for herself.

Tia Angelena was shocked and appalled that such a lady should have seen her in such a situation, and that she, of all people, would take it upon herself to nurse her back to health.

Nothing much was said, but the two always spoke in passing, and Tia Angelena did not forget.

Del Campo and Polanco had stopped by for a glass of wine, and Tia leaned her great forearms upon the bar and looked at them. She took the cigar from her teeth and said, "You work for the Malibu?"

"We do."

"It is between us, this."

"Sí?"

"The Señora is my friend."

She sensed their doubt, recognized their politeness, and said, "No matter . . . when I was dying, she cared for me. I have not forgotten."

Del Campo nodded. Who could forget such a thing? And the Señora had cared for this one? It was another good mark for her.

"She is our friend also," Del Campo said gently. "She is a woman, that one."

"Two men come here."

Polanco shrugged. "It is possible."

"Two men . . . they come, they go. I think they hide in the chaparral. They come when no one is near. When someone comes, they go."

"These men have names?"

She shrugged. "One is called Beltran."

"Ah?" Del Campo scratched his jaw. "I know this one. You are right, Tia, he is a bad man, a very bad man. When he comes, someone dies."

He paused for a moment. "And the other one? He is thin, hard? With greasy eyes that slide but never look at one?"

"Sí."

"It is Velasco.'

"You know them?" Polanco asked.

"From Chihuahua I know them, from Sonora I hear of them. I think it is very good you tell us, Tia."

"Why not? If they are proper bandits they will come here to drink, to laugh, to dance, to play at cards, and then vanish when the *soldados* come. But these? I think it is something they plan to do, you see? Something for which they must not be seen.

"I ask myself why this is so? I think of the Señora and Wooston, and I wonder."

"*Gracias,* Tia." Del Campo drew on his gauntlets. "Finish your wine, Polanco. I think we will ride."

A cool breeze came in off the blue water, a breeze that stirred the leaves of the old sycamore, lingered among the stiffer leaves of the oaks. The breeze cooled the water in the *ollas* that hung from the porch beams, stirred the lines of peppers hanging from strings along the porch.

A horse stamped in the corral, then blew dust from his nostrils. In the chaparral, a dove called.

The two vaqueros rode into the ranchyard on lathered horses. They swung down and Del Campo went to the door. "Señora?"

She came from within the cool house, and they explained. She listened, then shook her head. "He is gone. He rode out this morning to find the body of the Old One, to bury it. He is miles away by now."

"We must follow, then."

Montero came from the corral. "Stay," he said. "He wished to ride alone. He spoke to me of this." He hesitated. "I think it is something between the Old One and him."

"But if they come?"

167

"There is the Señora. We must think of her."

Johnny Mims came up from the bunkhouse they had built from the poles and tules left from the fandango. "He told us he wanted to ride alone."

Mims took tobacco from his pocket and filled his pipe. "You boys stay here. Won't do no good to kill him 'less they get her, too. Me an' my friends, we'll sort of trail over to Auntie's place and scout for some sign. If they been comin' down, they been leavin' signs. We'll scatter around and find them . . . or wait for them."

"But if they follow him?" Polanco protested.

"They take their own chances," Larkin Campbell said. "I rode with him a time or two. Ain't nobody comin' up on him."

Saddling up, the three rode down the trail. After all, a visit to a cantina was in order. And if those two showed up?

Johnny Mims had no doubts about that. If they showed up.

Sean Mulkerin rode easy in the saddle. This route was not the one he had followed before. Riding rough country where a man had enemies, it wasn't a good idea to become too familiar along the same trail. This time he crossed over the eastern flank of the Topatopa Mountains, watered his horse and made camp at Ten Sycamore Flat, and thought out his route. Riding alone toward a known destination was easier than scouting a doubtful trail for the first time.

He let his horse graze, watered it again, and then went back into the rocks of Red Reef Canyon and holed up in a hollow with an overhang of rocks. If anybody was following him, he could see them first from there.

Nothing in his life had given him confidence in his hold upon the future. All he had learned indicated that one lived by avoiding trouble, or if it could not be avoided, seeing it first.

To a wandering man in the wilderness a back trail must be as important as that ahead, for it might be the direction to be taken tomorrow, and when one faced around the trail looked far, far different. Gigantic boulders seen from one direction might be low, flat rocks seen from another . . . all things were different. Studying trails had taught him much about life, that much depends on the viewpoint.

They had been followed before, so why not again?

A deer came to the water to drink, then another and another. Sean Mulkerin lay quiet and watched. He had meat enough, and no desire to kill or to fire a shot, and if somebody was coming they would be apt to hear it before he did, although he was a man who watched his horse. A mustang was like any other wild creature and alert to sounds and sights, as wary as a deer and even more difficult to approach.

He slept, awakened, slept again. All was quiet. Only the rustling leaves of the sycamore, their mottled trunks ghostly in the night. At daybreak, after a brief scouting around, he moved out.

He rode no trail, but scouted his own way through the brush, studying the terrain before him for obstacles that must be skirted. As always there were canyons cut by runoff water, and these must be skirted or a way found into and out of them. The sky was cloudless, so entering them disturbed him not at all. What runoff there was came from the mountain right above him, so there could be no surprises. Often distant rains would start flash floods down canyons that would suddenly appear out of nowhere in the desert, miles from there, with a hot sun overhead. The wilderness delighted in surprises.

The sun was high in the sky when he topped out on the mesa above Beartrap Creek. From that vantage point he could look right into the open mouth of the great horseshoe of mountain that his mother had described.

From this distance it resembled any other mountain, dry, pine-clad, and rocky. He studied it for sometime with the telescope brought from the *Lady Luck*, but it told him nothing.

He walked his horse forward, and drawing up in the shade of some pines where the outline of his horse was lost in the shadows, he took a long time to survey the area before him. He would camp down there tonight, somewhere between Beartrap and Reyes creeks and tomorrow morning he would go into the horseshoe, find the cave, and if the Old One still lay there, he would bury him.

Sean put his hand to the butt of the Paterson. It was still there. And the Colt revolving rifle was also. He started his horse down a steep slide among the pines and within the hour had discovered what he wanted, a level place among the pines with a view into the hollow beyond. It was above Reyes Creek and in a small cove of about two acres.

He watered his horse in the creek, then rode back up and picketed it on the grass. Building his fire under a tree where the rising smoke would be dissipated by the branches and leaves, he prepared a small meal of broiled beef, the last of his tortillas, and coffee.

When he had eaten he put out his fire and moved back against the rock face where some trees offered shelter. After a glance at the sky he rigged a lean-to of branches and bark from a dead tree.

"Lost him," Beltran swore in short, bitter words. "We clean lost him."

Velasco shrugged. "What of it? He must go to the place of which Francisco spoke. There will be tracks. If he has taken another way, he still must come there. We will go there and wait."

"All right," Beltran said grudgingly, "only I don't see how he got away from us."

"He is a bad one, this," Velasco said. "I think it is better we ride carefully."

Beltran had been thinking the same thing. Of course, they had taken too much for granted. They knew where the man was going, so they had ignored tracks until suddenly realizing that there were none. Already they had been out longer than expected. Beltran was hoping Mulkerin carried enough grub. Then they would not have to go hungry on the way back.

When they found the place where the Señora had left her horse, they scouted carefully around. No one had been there for days.

Francisco had ridden away, and returned to see King-Pin go into the hollow. It must be that one they now looked at. "So?" Beltran said. "What is it? Just some other hills?"

"I heard something," Velasco said suddenly. "It was when we drank wine at the cantina. I heard the woman speak of this Russell. He was a young man when he rode out, but an old, old man when they found him again."

"Bah! It is foolishness! Woman's stories!"

"Perhaps. It is a thing to think of."

"Run out of water . . . thirst will do that to a man."

"Not as this one. He was truly *old* . . . in the space of one week, or less. I do not know how long."

"Forget it."

Beltran did not like to talk of such things, nor to think of them. It was all nonsense, of course.

With rifles in their hands they settled down to wait.

It was just before nightfall when they moved into position, and Sean Mulkerin had just gone to sleep. His camp was above and behind them but not over six hundred yards away.

Sean was awakened by the restlessness of his horse. His eyes opened, and he listened, watching the gray gelding he had ridden on this ride. Its head was up, ears pointed. Nostrils flaring, it looked off to the south.

Sean got quietly to his feet. "What is it, boy? What's the trouble?"

The gelding twitched at the touch of his hand, then turned its nose toward him. He rubbed the nose affectionately. "Something down there that bothers you, is there? Is it a cat?"

The gray tossed its head as if understanding but disputing the point. "All right, what do you say if we move out now? I've had some sleep, and you're not going to get much worrying this way."

Swiftly, he saddled up, gathered his few belongings, and stepped into the saddle.

He rode off the mesa on an angle, descended into Reyes Creek and watered his horse. The horse had sunk its muzzle into the shallow stream when suddenly its head came up.

"Steady, boy! Steady!" Sean whispered.

Dimly, through the trees, he could see movement. A horse! No . . . two horses.

Fortunately, the bottom at that point was sandy so no hoof would click on stone. He walked his horse across and was up the bank and into the trees before he heard a horse whinny behind him!

He dropped quickly to the ground and held his own horse's nose. "No, boy, *no!*" he whispered.

He waited, heard some vague muttering, and after a moment a man appeared from the trees where he had seen the horses. He could make him out only as an indistinct figure and largely because of the gray or white pants he wore.

Sean waited, his left hand holding the horse, his right on the pommel ready to mount. After a moment the man disappeared and Sean mounted and walked his horse up the narrow opening along the creek.

All was quiet, only the rustle of water from the small creek, probably dry most of the year. He rode on, then came to a point where he had to walk. Dismounting, he tied his horse and went on up the hollow on foot.

Suddenly, he saw on his left the flat place of which his mother had spoken. He walked out to it and stood there, waiting. Nothing happened.

The moon was rising.

Once he thought he heard a vague stirring around him, but he remained still. He could see the dark mouth of the cave.

Suddenly a voice spoke. "You have come for gold?"

"No," he replied quietly, "an Old One was left unburied here. He had no son to bury him, so I have come."

"There is no need." The voice sounded strangely hollow as though the person spoke down a well. "He has been cared for."

"Nevertheless, I must see for myself."

"Who are the two men beyond the portals?"

"I believe them to be enemies, but I have not seen

173

them." Sean paused. "No doubt they will be waiting when I go out."

"You are not afraid?"

"Of them? No."

"Not them, but of this place?"

"No."

"You do not wish to come through?"

Sean paused. "Through? No, I am content with what is here."

"So be it."

There was no further sound, and no more of the voice. Sean waited, then went back to the rocks and sat down. He leaned his head back and looked at the stars. Was he afraid?

No.

The Old One had taught him that. One need not be afraid. Fear was a thing of the mind, and if one did not offer it a place, it had none.

He must have dozed, for the dawn was suddenly there, and he arose swiftly and went into the cave.

There was no body. It was as Russell had said, the Old One was gone.

On the shelf was the row of jars . . . four of them.

His mother had said there were *five*.

He looked into each one, and each one was empty.

But one was gone . . . *where?*

Chapter 20

Glancing quickly around, Sean saw nothing of the missing jar, but it was of small matter. He was finished here. Sometime it would be good to return and look around more carefully.

It was obvious that work had been done here, very ancient work, for the marks of chisels and picks were apparent.

Sean walked outside. For a moment he stood looking around but there was nobody in sight. As a matter of fact, he had expected no one. Men could come and go in these hills easily enough, for there were cracks in the rocks, tumbled boulders, clumps of brush and trees.

He did not even wonder about the voice. Was that because of something the Old One had taught him? Or was it simply that he respected the desire for privacy on the part of the Indians or whoever they were? In any event, the Old One had been cared for and his body disposed of in a manner fitting to his nature.

Sean stood for a moment on the terrace and said quietly, "Good-bye, then," and walked away.

He had no illusions. Whoever those men had been, the chances were they would be waiting outside the hollow.

If they were chance travelers they would be gone, but he had no such notion. That they were here, at this time, was too much of a coincidence.

He went into the brush near the trail, paused to listen, heard nothing, and went on, as soundlessly as possible. To follow the trail itself seemed at this moment to be less than wise.

When he had gone almost to where he had left his horse, he paused. This would be the first of the crucial spots. If they had found his horse they would be waiting for him to return to it, and if they had not they would be waiting outside the hollow.

He listened, but heard no sound. Not even that of birds or insects. For some reason they avoided this place. He started on, then paused. He was now on the edge of a small clearing. Three paths pointing toward a place among the trees, a flat stone lay across two other stones, and the three paths met at this stone table.

The altar! This was the place of which Russell had spoken.

He walked toward it, checking the ground as he went. He could see the boot tracks left by Russell, some of them smudged by the tracks of sandals . . . not moccasins, but sandals.

The altar stone was smooth as if polished or worn from much use . . . what use? He looked carefully around. The place was in no way distinguished except by the stone table and by the converging trails.

Turning, he walked away. He was now within no more than fifteen or twenty yards of his horse. He found an opening in the brush, and touching not so much as a leaf, he sidled through, eased himself past a clump of manzanita.

Sean Mulkerin could see the horse was dozing, quiet, unalarmed. Yet he waited, letting his eyes and his senses feel out the situation. He scanned the trees nearby.

A bird was scratching at something in the dust, a squirrel was high on a branch opposite, busy on some activity of his own. All was quiet.

Rifle in hand, he worked through the brush to his horse, gathered the reins but did not mount. Instead, he turned toward the opening of the hollow carrying his rifle in one hand, leading his horse.

"Quiet now, boy," he whispered.

In his mind he tried to picture the trail up which he had come. It would point him right at their camp, and a good man with a rifle would have him dead to rights. He considered what lay to right and left. Correctly, right was his way to go, but opposite the opening of the cul-de-sac there had been a dry water course on his left while the small stream took a sharp bend to the right before joining Reyes Creek.

He walked on, hesitated, listening. Hearing nothing he went on again. Then he crossed over the trail and the trickle of water and went into the trees and boulders west of the trail. It was rough going, but he found a thread of deer trail and followed it.

He glanced up at the walls. He was at the end, the towering shoulders of the mountain reared up at the very opening, one close above him, the other a couple of hundred yards off. His eyes searched the place where their camp had been and he saw nothing.

He looked carefully around, still nothing. He moved on, tiptoeing among the rocks, careful to disturb no stone or pebble. Suddenly the dry water course was there, on his left, and at the same moment, he saw them.

They were fifty yards away, and spread out, watching the opening.

As his eyes found them, Velasco's head turned. The man was quick as a cat. As his eyes touched Sean's, Velasco reacted. He spun and fired!

The bullet smashed into the rock at Sean's feet and Sean's gun lifted.

He fired, the Colt jumped in his hands and shifting his aim by a hair he fired again. The second bullet caught Velasco and the man stumbled, then went to the ground.

Not dead . . . perhaps not even wounded badly, judging by the way he went down.

The other man had disappeared like a shadow, and Sean moved, working his way back through the brush, leading his horse. He found a place in the dry water course where some slabs of rock offered shelter for his horse, and he tied it to some brush there, loosely, in case he got hit. If he was killed he did not want the horse left there to die.

Crouching, he worked his way back through the brush and up through the trees, trying for a better position.

Suddenly there was a sharp *whsst* in the air and a loop dropped over his shoulders. His eyes followed the rope as the roper jerked. It was Velasco, but the Colt rifle was still in Sean's hands and he fired from waist level. The Mexican jerked on the riata but a second too late, for the heavy slug caught him in the chest.

His great dark eyes wide, Velasco took a staggering step forward, then half-turned and fell, sprawling upon the rocks.

Sean Mulkerin shook off the rope and crouched down beside a rock.

The other man would have heard the shots. By now he would be wondering what had happened.

Sean drew back slowly, keeping the body of Velasco in view, and he waited.

The shadow of a rock indicated the passing of time, and he noted its position.

A bird was twittering in a tree, a squirrel scurried nearby, but there was no other sound. The dry water course in which he found himself was probably just runoff from the rocks, and not what he had suspected. It was probably dead-ended not far back. It was not the water course he had originally noted. That one was further along the mountain.

He must be careful. Such a mistake could be fatal.

He shifted hands on his rifle, drying his palms on his shirt front. It was getting very hot.

He waited, liking his position less and less, yet fearing

to move. So often in such a deadly game the first to move was the first to die. He turned his head, scanning the wall of the mountain. Sweat trickled into his eyes. He lifted a hand to mop his brow and a bullet spat rock fragments that stung his face.

Sean dropped on his side and rolled, coming up on his knees. Another bullet struck just before him but he leaped up and ran right out of the mouth of the wash and ducked left into the trees. A gun blasted almost in his ears, and he saw a man crouched, thumbing a load into his rifle.

They saw each other at the same instant and the man dropped his rifle and powder horn and grabbed for the pistol at his belt.

Sean Mulkerin seized the moment. His Colt rifle came up waist high and he squeezed off his shot. Not twenty yards separated them and the chance of missing was slight, yet he took just that instant to make sure as the other man's gun was clearing the holster.

The Colt rifle leaped in his hands, and Beltran's mouth dropped open in a wide O of surprise and shock. He took a step forward, his fingers spreading wide as he dropped his pistol. He fell, and as he fell, Sean fired again.

The body jerked with the impact, and then lay still. Sean waited a minute, watching the body, and when there was no movement he went forward and kicked the gun away.

He went through the dead man's pockets. Several gold pieces and a small bit of torn paper, evidently carried for some time, on it the one word *Wooston*.

Sean Mulkerin returned to his horse, and mounting up he rode back along the trail. It was a long ride home, but his horse was tough and in good shape and if he pushed it . . . .

Moonlight lay wide upon the Pacific when the trail he had taken led him down to the beach. Despite the presence of Mims and his friends, Sean was worried. Wooston was shrewd, a man whose cunning had no limits, and he was relentless in his pursit of a goal.

All was quiet. The surf rolled lightly upon the sand, and off shore he could see a light from the *Lady Luck*, reassuring in its peaceful look.

His horse's hoofs made almost no sound upon the wet sand, and the tracks he left would be gone by daybreak. Despite the calm of the night, he was uneasy, and even the lights of the *Lady Luck* did not calm him.

He turned off the beach and started up the road to the ranch. He was tired. He had ridden hard these last two days, and far into the night. The thought of his own bed awaiting him was all that kept him going, and the chance to see his mother and Mariana.

He held his Colt rifle in his hands as he rode into the ranchyard. It was long after midnight and all was dark and quiet. That was as it should be, and talking could wait until daylight. He would just—

He had started to swing down and he was moving when the bullets struck him. His leg was lifted to swing back over the saddle when the windows of his house seemed to rip apart with flame. He felt a heavy blow in the side, another on the skull. He felt himself falling, heard the thunder of the guns die away, and he was lying sprawled on the hard clay where he had played as a child.

He had been hit hard, but he was conscious. A wild wave of fear swept through him. Was this how it felt to die? Was he going to die? Were they going to win after all?

He heard heavy steps crossing the yard, steps that stopped, then a heavy boot kicked him in the ribs, and then the same boot turned him over.

"Is he dead?" It sounded like the voice of Fernandez.

"Are you crazy? With seven of us shootin' at him? Look at him! Blood all over and his skull ripped open!"

"Let's get him out of the way before she comes." That was Tomas.

"Hell, let him lay! When she sees him she'll throw herself off her horse and run right to him. Just what we want. It'll be night to daylight then and she'll be right in our sights."

"She's got friends," Tomas warned.

"So've I. Better friends. Nick Bell said he'd say that Beltran an' Velasco did it."

"What about them?"

"Hell, Mulkerin's here, ain't he? If they was alive, he wouldn't be, you can bet on that. I don't know what happened, but he's done them in. Let's get out of sight. She might be early."

They walked back to the house.

For the first time he felt pain . . . and sickness, a terrible, terrible sickness. He was bleeding. His skull was burst, they said. And maybe it was.

He had to warn them. For some reason his mother, and perhaps Mariana, had left the ranch. For some reason Mims was not here, and if Montero was here he was dead or a prisoner.

Prisoner? Not likely. Not Wooston. If Montero was here, he was dead.

What of Polanco and Del Campo?

He lay perfectly still, fighting off the weakness that enveloped him. He dug his fingers into the clay. He must live! He must! He could not die! Not until he had warned them.

By some trick Wooston had got them all to leave and had occupied the ranch and now he was waiting. After the killings he would simply leave the bodies, appear where he could be seen, and nothing could be proved.

Captain Nick Bell would make sure that nothing could be proved. There might be mutterings, but Bell was the law. An appeal could only be made to Micheltorena and he would not interfere.

Sean Mulkerin had been hit hard. He was hurt, and he must have appeared dying or dead or they would have shot him again. He dug his fingers into the earth and fought bitterly, desperately against the tides of pain.

He must somehow be alive when his mother came home. His gun was in its holster. When he had been hit he had been dismounting and his rifle must have flown from his hands. The gelding had run off.

Wooston and his men had gone back into the house. He struggled against the weakness. With his fingers he inched himself along. The effort left him gasping and empty. He fought against a wave of nausea. Slowly, carefully he willed his right leg to move out from the line of his body, and slowly, it moved.

That leg was not broken then. Bleeding, yes. He could feel wetness inside his pant leg. Slowly, he tried to move his left leg, nothing happened. He tried again . . . nothing.

Six feet away on his right was the beginning of a wash cut by runoff water. If he could get into that—

But they would see he was gone and come at once. He lay still, fighting the sickness and trying to think. His head was throbbing with pain, his left leg was numb.

On his right, along the edge of the wash, were some rocks, a dozen of them as large as his head, placed there in a row to mark the edge of the wash and where his mother had at one time planned a flower garden.

Reaching out slowly with his left hand he rolled one of those stones nearer. From the house they would be unlikely to see anything but the dark bulk of his body. He rolled the stone even with his head. Slowly, he edged his body to his right, then rolled that stone back and another in line with his head.

After that he lay still, eyes closed, too weak to move. After a long time he fought another stone into place, and worked a little further toward the edge. He had now moved nearly two feet, and had the fourth stone in place, hoping they would mistake the stones for his body and not come to look.

Why were they so sure his mother would return now? Were they tricking her into coming back now? What was happening?

Somewhere along the line, he passed out, and when he was conscious again he had a throb of pain in his head, another in his side, and a stiffness and agony in his left leg.

He lay very still. Somehow he had rolled over on his back and was staring up into a starlit sky. The moon was gone. He lay very still, trying to breathe slowly and carefully, fighting by sheer will to get his mind to working.

He had been out cold. Now he was aware again. But how long before his mother came? How much time did he have?

He tried to move his left leg, but it felt heavy and awkward, the muscles refused to respond. Using his right hand he pushed himself up a little and managed to roll over. Now he was within inches of the wash.

After a struggle, he got his hand on another stone and rolled it into line. Slowly then, he eased himself back into the wash and lowered his head to the sand. For a long time he lay there, knowing such weakness as he had never imagined, his head throbbing heavily with a dull, solid pounding. His side seemed wet, and when he touched himself there a spasm of pain went through him.

He looked around for his rifle, but could make out nothing but the deep shadows in the wash and the vague light in the ranch yard, light from the stars overhead.

They should be coming soon, and he must be awake. He must be ready to warn them. He must be ready to shoot.

Over and over he said it in his mind. He lay gasping slowly, heavily. He desperately wanted a drink, and the thought of the *ollas* hanging under the porch was almost more than he could bear. There they were, gallons of cold, clear water.

There was water at the trough near the corral, too, but that was far, far away, beyond the limit of what strength he had left.

Suddenly his eyes were open and he was aware that he had been asleep without remembering even closing his eyes. He listened . . . somebody in the house was talking.

He could make out none of the words.

He blinked his eyes . . . why, it wasn't in the house! It was there! Right in front of him.

His mother was on a horse and someone was beside her. It was Mariana.

Someone was talking.

"He's dead, and we killed him." Wooston suddenly stepped from under the overhang. "Look for yourself. He's there!"

He stepped out another step and pointed at the rocks. Suddenly, as the skies had paled somewhat since he had gone inside, he seemed to see the rocks for the first time.

Unbelieving Wooston took a step forward and Sean

grabbed the bank and pulled himself erect. He grabbed a stick and using it for a staff, propped himself up. His gun was in his right hand.

"Not yet, Wooston. I'm not dead yet."

With an animallike cry, Wooston swung his gun up as Fernandez ran from the house. Sean shot, firing quickly but smoothly.

Wooston wore a white shirt and the target was perfect. Fernandez ran into the open and began firing rapidly. Bullets dusted around Sean but suddenly somebody else was shooting and then another. Sean shot Fernandez and saw the man fall.

Tomas Alexander suddenly appeared in the door, his hands up.

The shooting was over, and all was still.

Sean Mulkerin stood weaving on his feet, staring around him, and then he had two women holding him and crying, and Johnny Mims was riding into the yard with Honeycutt and Campbell.

Chapter 21

Sean Mulkerin had been in bed three weeks when Andres Machado came to see him.

Mariana opened the door for him, and Machado stepped in. "So?" he said. "You choose this way of escape! Anything to avoid fighting Machado! You go out and get yourself shot by a pack of dogs! Well, so be it. I shall have to wait."

"Sorry, my friend," Sean said, smiling a little. "First time I can ever remember keeping any man waiting, but I guess it will have to be."

Machado walked closer to the bed. "My friend, you

185

are a brave man, a very brave man. I am sorry that my anger would not let me think wisely.

"You were right, of course! Why waste time on a girl who does not love me when so many do? Of course, it is true! I shall stay here awhile, and then I shall go back to Mexico, but I shall miss you, my friend."

Sean held out his hand. "You're a tough enemy, amigo, but you'll make a better friend."

When he was gone, Sean closed his eyes. He could hear the voices outside, the soft murmur of them, slowly receding as they drew away from the house.

His eyes closed. It was good to rest, and he would have to rest a great deal. He had been hit three times, and he had lost blood.

The curtain stirred. He heard his mother's voice outside. She was talking again of planting flowers where the stones were . . . how many times had she planned that?

Michael was coming out. He was back from Monterey. Things were happening and there was talk of a rebellion against Micheltorena.

Suddenly his muscles tensed, then slowly, very slowly they relaxed. His eyes closed. Somebody was in the room with him, somebody who moved very, very softly. He thought something brushed against the bed, he thought someone leaned above him, then a faint click of a stone on stone and a faint shuffling.

Under the blankets his fingers closed around the butt of his Paterson. He waited, but there was no further sound, nothing but a faint, lingering smell of crushed cedar.

Suddenly someone was singing outside, then Mariana came in. She stopped suddenly, and he opened his eyes. His mother was behind her and they were staring with eyes that would not believe.

He lifted himself up and looked.

On the mantle above the fireplace was the missing jar from the cave in the mountains.

The Señora crossed to the mantle and started to pick it up. Then with both hands she lifted it down. It seemed to be heavy . . . quite heavy.

She looked within. "It's gold," she said, her voice trembling a little with surprise. "It's gold, Sean."

He lay back and closed his eyes. "Wherever you are . . . whoever you are . . . thanks."

Historical Note

This is a fictional story of the Malibu coast and some of the mountains that lie inland.

Shortly after the period of this story the people of California rebelled against Micheltorena and he was expelled from the province. His place was taken by Pio Pico.

Many of the names along the coast *were* given by an unknown people before the coming of the Chumash. Who these people were we do not know.

There were two peoples before the Chumash of whom we know a little: the Oak Grove people, and the Hunting people who followed them. The Chumash seem to have been an intelligent, generally well-built people whose boats show considerable sophistication, and judging by their construction, the Chumash must have been skilled in rough seas and landings through the surf.

Actually the Chumash area extended from Malibu and perhaps Topanga to the vicinity of San Luis Obispo, and inland beyond the Cuyama River, Pine Mountain, and Mt. Pinos.

Presumably the first man to own the Malibu was Jose Bartolome Tapia, a colonist who came north with de Anza in 1775. The grant was made about 1802. In 1848 the Malibu was sold to a young Frenchman, Leon Victor Prudhomme who married a daughter of Tiburcio Tapia.

In 1857, with the title in question, Prudhomme sold the Malibu to an Irishman, Matthew Keller, for ten cents an acre. Thirty-four years later his son sold the place for ten dollars an acre, and the Malibu comprised 13,316 acres. The buyer was Frederick Rindge, who had found his dream home and lived many happy years on the rancho, leaving it to his wife, May Rindge.

The story of her defense of the property against the oncoming tide of highway and subdivision is an epic in itself, too long to be entered into here.

Before the tides of change few things remain the same, and the shores of Malibu are crowded with the homes of motion picture and television stars. Further along there are beaches, motels, restaurants, and cottages.

Behind them are the mountains. Roads now cross these mountains and wind along their flanks, yet isolated spots remain, unchanged in the passing of years. The graves of the earlier peoples have often been looted by the unthinking, destroying any chance of proper dating, and vandals have marred cave paintings left by the Chumash.

When people from Los Angeles "go to the snow" it is often to the vicinity of Pine Mountain, but the hollow where lay the Old One's cave is as it was, unchanged from one hundred, perhaps one thousand or ten thousand years ago.

Only do not look for the cave. You might find it.

About Louis L'Amour

"I think of myself in the oral tradition—as a troubadour, a village taleteller, the man in the shadows of the campfire. That's the way I'd like to be remembered—as a storyteller. A good storyteller."

It is doubtful that any author could be as at home in the world recreated in his novels as Louis Dearborn L'Amour. Not only could he physically fill the boots of the rugged characters he wrote about, but he literally "walked the land my characters walk." His personal experiences as well as his lifelong devotion to historical research combined to give Mr. L'Amour the unique knowledge and understanding of people, events, and the challenge of the American frontier that became the hallmarks of his popularity.

Of French-Irish descent, Mr. L'Amour could trace his own family in North America back to the early 1600s and follow their steady progression westward, "always on the frontier." As a boy growing up in Jamestown, North Dakota, he absorbed all he could about his family's frontier heritage, including the story of his great-grandfather who was scalped by Sioux warriors.

Spurred by an eager curiosity and desire to broaden his horizons, Mr. L'Amour left home at the age of fifteen and enjoyed a wide variety of jobs including seaman, lumberjack, elephant handler, skinner of dead cattle, assessment miner, and officer on tank destroyers during World War II. During his "yondering" days he also circled the world on a freighter, sailed a dhow on the Red Sea, was shipwrecked in the West Indies and stranded in the Mojave Desert. He won fifty-one of fifty-nine fights as a professional boxer and worked as a journalist and lecturer. He was a voracious reader and collector of rare books. His personal library contained 17,000 volumes.

Mr. L'Amour "wanted to write almost from the time I could talk." After developing a widespread following for his many frontier and adventure stories written for fiction magazines, Mr. L'Amour published his first full-length novel, *Hondo*, in the United States in 1953. Every one of his more than 100 books is in print; there are nearly 230 million copies of his books in print worldwide, making him one of the bestselling authors in modern literary history. His books have been translated into twenty languages, and more than forty-five of his novels and stories have been made into feature films and television movies.

His hardcover bestsellers include *The Lonesome Gods, The Walking Drum* (his twelfth-century historical novel) *Jubal Sackett, Last of the Breed,* and *The Haunted Mesa.* His memoir, *Education of a Wandering Man,* was a leading bestseller in 1989. Audio dramatizations and adaptations of many L'Amour stories are available on cassette tapes from Bantam Audio Publishing.

The recipient of many great honors and awards, in 1983 Mr. L'Amour became the first novelist ever to be awarded the National Gold Medal by the United States Congress in honor of his life's work. In 1984 he was also awarded the Medal of Freedom by President Reagan.

Louis L'Amour died on June 10, 1988. His wife, Kathy, and their two children, Beau and Angelique, carry the L'Amour tradition forward with new books written by the author during his lifetime to be published by Bantam well into the nineties.

LOUIS L'AMOUR

BANTAM'S #1
ALL-TIME BESTSELLING AUTHOR
AMERICA'S FAVORITE FRONTIER WRITER

LOUIS L'AMOUR

BANTAM'S #1
ALL-TIME BESTSELLING AUTHOR
AMERICA'S FAVORITE FRONTIER WRITER